REALM: RULER OF THE PEOPLE, GOD OF DEATH

Book 2 of the Realm Saga

By: Jessica Cantwell

The tales of Pushkar Lake, Brahma the Hindu God of Creation, his wife Saraswati and Manu as told in this book, "Realm: Ruler of the People, God of Death," should not be misinterpreted as fact. The storylines surrounding them in the Realm Saga are strictly fiction, created for the equally fictional dimension of Realm. It's invention; the characters of Realm and plot are all fantasy made up for your enjoyment. This book is a work of fiction. The characters and story lines have been created purely by the author's imagination for your enjoyment. Any resemblance to any person, living or dead, or any events or occurrences, is purely coincidental.

The true stories about Pushkar Lake, Brahma, Saraswati and Manu can be found on the Internet or you can try to find out more about them at your local library.

This book is dedicated to my oldest, my boy, my love.
"Bruh!"

Contents:

THE KING

Chapter One
Drained

"Your Majesty?"

"What is it, Mackinnley?"

"My Lord, what has become of you? You're much too tired – withering away before my very eyes - look at you – you're drained!"

"News flash, Mackinnley! Tell me something I don't know."

"Oh, this can wait. You need rest! I won't bother you...."

"Yet you already have!"

"Yes... yes sire – true, you have me there - yet completely unintentional it was...."

"Is!"

"I see your point – yes – very well...."

"And yours? Will you be getting to it any time soon, Mackinnley?"

"My what sir?"

"POINT! POINT! The reason you are disturbing me so!"

"Yes, I – I just thought you'd be happy to know your new shipment is on its way."

"Indeed. How many will I receive this time?"

"Two dozen. And we have more signing up every day."

"Hah! I knew it. Does anyone suspect...."

"Not a thing!"

"Magnificent! Mackinnley, that is the best news I've heard all day!"

"Yes – yes sire, I thought it might be. Sire? SIRE? THE GROUND! WE MUST GET YOU SOMEWHERE SAFE!"

"Relax, it's not at all what it appears to be. Things seldom are. This here is no ordinary quake."

"How can you be so sure, my Lord?"

"Because, nineteen years ago I created it."

"You created a quake?"

"Nineteen years - I can't quite believe it's taken this long – hmmm, I wonder...."

"What are you saying, sir?"

"YOU FOOL! WHAT DO YOU THINK I SPEAK OF?"

"Could it be? After all this time?"

"Could it be? Could it be? YOU NITWIT, WHAT ELSE DO YOU SUPPOSE IT IS?"

"Ah? Uh?...."

"Ah, hah! Look at her, Mackinnley! My beautiful Daviana has come back to me. Ha, ha, ha, ha, ha - My darling! Oh, how I've waited for the day you would return to me."

"Sire? Sire? – You – you do know she can't hear you, right?"

"OF COURSE, I KNOW SHE CAN'T HEAR ME! SHE'S A STATUE FOR CRYING OUT LOUD! WHAT KIND OF BLUBBERING MORON DO YOU THINK I AM? TEARLACH! VILHELM! GATHER THE TROOPS, YOU HAVE WORK TO DO!"

"Yes, your Majesty."

"Mackinnley?"

"Master?"

"What a lovely day this has turned out to be!"

"Yes, yes - it most certainly has. Oh no! No sire! – You mustn't get up. You need to rest!"

"Hush now Mackinnley. Rest? Now? Why I have the strength of twenty men pulsating through my veins. Try and stop me! Daviana's return is the icing on my cake! Prepare the castle! Alert the kitchen! We shall have company any second, and I am feeling quite famished!"

LILY

Chapter Two
New Beginning

I often wonder how and why moods can change like the flip of a switch. One second I'm basking in the glory of what feels like perpetual elation, then CLICK, life kicks me in the groin!

Now I'm suffering a severe case of postpartum depression and again my mind wonders how I could get to such a place so quickly? Is it just me? Am I the only one that can snap in and out of a funk faster than a speeding bullet? Quicker than a ray of light?

Da – da – da – daah – na – na – na - naah!!!!! I'm Lily Monroe – Super mood swinging woman! Who needs Kryptonite when you have super human hormones like mine?

No seriously, how can one ebb and flow so rapidly without even allowing time for the transition? I spend more time thinking about it than my body allows for the flux. Really, when it comes down to it, it is an unbelievable superpower in and of itself. And just like the actual ability I do have, which is invisibility in case you didn't know, I have to learn how to control it.

It all started on March 25, 1992, when my mother and father were out strolling through Patterson Park, in Baltimore, Maryland, the town where I grew up. That night was a clear and crisp one, so I am told. Yet they managed to keep warm in each other's arms.

They hadn't known each other very long. A few days after Christmas a man stumbled through the doors of Johns Hopkins Hospital for a psychiatric evaluation, where my mother was interning. He was disoriented, grief-stricken and in need of help. One look into his vivid blue-green eyes and my mother was smitten. And when she took him by the hand, it was as if nothing else existed.

Instead of admitting him as a patient, she used an unorthodox approach and took him out for a cup of coffee. They talked all night. About what, I'll never know, for my mother would never disclose that information. Every time I ask her, her response is always the same ... doctor/patient confidentiality.

What I do know is that her unconventional cup of coffee that night offered up an accelerated, ground-breaking counseling session, which in turn led to her opening her own psychiatric rehabilitation center years later, called Revitalize.

But back then; in the early months of 1992 (the happiest months of my mother's life) these two strangers were no longer man and woman, patient and doctor. They became one. Hungry in love, they devoured every waking moment together - always thirsting for more.

It was that fire that kept them warm the night of March twenty-fifth. Blinded by love, oblivious to their surroundings, the two lovebirds happily frolicked through the quiet grounds of Patterson Park, playfully chasing one another around the dilapidated observatory. My mother vaguely remembers her fall. The sharp twist of her ankle followed by a small cry of pain.

From the moment she fell to the ground the events were a little bit foggy. She remembers my father running to her, kissing her forehead, whispering in her ear that she was all right. She let out an embarrassed giggle amidst dampened eyes while he caressed her ankle, rubbing it gently, bathing it with his sweet kisses.

The pain began to dissipate, replaced by a warm internal glow, much like the feeling you get after a glass of wine. She was drunk, drunk on love. That happy numbness was followed by ease. She felt so silly in that moment. One; for feeling confident enough to run in heels (because she never wears heels) and two; for overestimating her injury.

She stood without any discomfort and thanked him for coming to her rescue. A period of teasing ensued. Playful taunting followed by bouts of childish laughter. And when their giggling died down, they stood there gazing into each other's eyes. No words were exchanged. They already knew what one another was thinking, feeling....

My mother always tells me "There is no need for words when you're blessed with such emotional and psychological interaction. Chemistry, Lily, pure chemistry! One day you will meet a man who will ignite a spark within you. When that day arrives, you will understand the power of our affinity."

It was that chemistry which alerted my father to the presence of danger. For the look in my mother's eyes told him something was severely wrong. He did not turn to see the two men, dressed in black, standing behind him. He didn't need to survey the land to know that they were alone, cloaked in the black of night, cornered against the vandalized ramshackle building.

"I'm so sorry Orvah. Please forgive me," my father whispered. And that was it. The brisk assault was a blur. In the blink of an eye the two mysterious men vanished, taking my father along with them. Extinguishing their fire. My mother was left all alone and cold.

At first she stood frozen, too afraid to move. It was barely a minute before her fear turned to worry. Frantically she ran around the grounds, calling for him, to no avail. She alerted the police, filed a report about the attack. Every square inch of the park was searched, the skating rink, the boat lake, even the decaying pagoda. There was no sign of a struggle, no sign of my father. It was as if he had vanished into thin air. Better yet, since there was no record of anyone with his name residing in the Baltimore area, it was as if he never existed.

People around the neighborhood were beginning to think my mother was losing her mind. Blamed it on her spending too much time at that "looney bin" she liked to call work. My grandfather Mac was her biggest supporter. There was no doubt in his mind that the events of that night actually occurred. He led the search at the park himself and often returned to walk it alone. Come hell or high water he wouldn't give up until my mother blew the whistle.

People started to come around as time passed and my mother began to swell. When I arrived a little less than forty weeks later, on the first and coldest night of December, the gossip mill had laid the crazy talk to rest and rallied by her side in support. After all, this was Baltimore! She had a new bundle of joy to keep her busy and the search for my father came to an abrupt halt. One look into my eyes – his eyes - told her he was with her all along.

I would like to tell you my childhood was a normal one. For the most part it was. Grandmother, Grandpa Mac, Mom and I all resided in our cozy row house at number 6 Boyer Street, located in a small section of Baltimore known as Butcher's Hill. Together we were one happy family and from within the confines of our form-stone walls everything to me was picture perfect. Then again, I was just a child and when you're that young all of your life is seen from the inside out; and most of what you see are images and concepts created from the fantasy of your own foolish mind. Innocence mixed with pure imagination. Take my best friend Ina, for example!

It wasn't until I reached prepubescent adolescence that reality started to sink in and I became aware of how different my family and myself really were. Not until that point in time did it ever occur to me how unusual it was to have an imaginary friend until the age of eight.

After I was forced to stop playing with Ina little bits and pieces of real life started to infiltrate their way into my head. While walking with Mac it became clear. I was the only child not playing something. There I was eagerly learning about birds and vegetation while other children were running in circles trying to tag one another, kicking a ball around or climbing on the jungle gym. They were playing the kind of fun and games that I only experienced as part of our physical education curriculum at school.

And as much as I loved participating in those events I enjoyed Grandpa Mac's lessons a whole lot more. Sadly, it was during those times, while I was supposed to be learning about nature, that the outside started to seep in, and that is how I began perceiving my family and myself - from the outside in.

I noticed how I chose to occupy my free time wasn't the only thing that separated me from the other children. My family was whimsical. Recycling, raw-food-eating, incense-burning Hippies! No, that's not quite right. After all, they're not the acid-dropping beatniks with tie-dyed t-shirts and flip-flops. They're – well – naturalists. Plain and simple!

I watched children chowing down on over-processed foods. Cheeseburgers, hot dogs, potato chips, bologna sandwiches, chocolate bars and cotton candy, as I nibbled on organic carrots and cucumbers. Every smell wafted through my nostrils, danced on my taste buds, leaving me with temptation. I wanted to know what it was like to taste the salt, the grease and the sweet smell of candied sugar. I just had to!

It was at the age of twelve, after my grandmother fell ill, that I began trying to fit in. Easier said than done! I started pitching my homemade lunch for vending machine snacks. I would tell Mac I was going to the park to look for birds just to get the chance to jump on the jungle gym, but by then it was too late. The kids my age had moved on to something new like group dates at the movie theatre and slumber parties. I stood out like a sore thumb. And it wasn't just because I was old enough to babysit for half of the kids on the playground that I still pathetically roamed. It was because I was taller, skinnier and paler than everyone else my age.

And when I say paler I truly mean it. Every inch of my hair and skin, head to toe, is the whitest shade of white. Platinum! Yet I'm not an albino, which all of my classmates at school assume I am. They are too thick-headed to know that unlike an albino I have plenty of pigment in my naturally berry-stained lips and my razor-sharp aquamarine eyes.

Come to find out, my eyes completely freak them out too. Most of the population has brown. We've all seen shades of blue, hazel, even green and black. But to match the blue green waters of the Caribbean Sea is something you only get when wearing colored contact lenses, which I don't!

Elizabeth Taylor had violet eyes, another rarity, and was labeled a bombshell, so I hold out hope for myself. Yet I couldn't argue that at twelve years old. I doubt anyone else my age even knew who she was.

I doubt anyone else my age was reading Marion Zimmer Bradley's "Mists of Avalon" or Michael Crichton's "Jurassic Park," which is precisely what I did when my Grandmother could no longer leave her bed.

My days of roaming Patterson Park trying to gain acceptance dissolved into hours upon hours of round-the-clock care giving, which I was more than happy to do. At Grandma's bedside, I pored through fantasy novels, memoirs and biographies of some of her favorite celebrities: Marilyn Monroe, Judy Garland, John F. Kennedy and of course, Elizabeth Taylor.

Yet, no matter how content I felt at home, it all changed the moment my toe hit the front stoop of the house. Like putting a wool sweater over sensitive skin, I was instantly agitated, my curiosity merely scratching the surface of my displeasure.

So naturally one day while returning books to the library I stopped to do something I had never done before. I roamed through the cinema section, reading title upon title of blockbuster hits and television series. I searched through the children's movie section combing over every cartoon character, every Disney masterpiece.

A feeling like no other began to rise up into the pit of my stomach. I was angry, jealous and sad that my family would allow me to miss out on such normal childhood entertainment, for we have never owned a television. After that I stormed through the whole foods store gathering the items on the list I had been given that morning, then stomped into the nearest fast food restaurant and ordered a cheeseburger off the dollar menu.

Although I had been deceiving my family by gorging on pretzels and potato chips at school this was downright defiant. That first bite of meat was so irresistible I dare say I wanted another, but knew full well not to spend any more of Grandpa Mac's money than I already had.

From that moment on the floodgates were open and after Grandma passed I had the time and freedom to secretly drown my sorrows in vats of greasy goodness. And that is precisely what I did up until my mother admitted herself as a patient into her own psychiatric rehabilitation center.

Again, the neighborhood busybodies exploded with your run of the mill grapevine gossip and when it got right down to the root of things, no one was left rallying at our side anymore. Orla had died, Orvah was crazy, Mac was distant and Lily was downright weird.

I was sad, angry, confused, depressed and most of all lonely. Food became my only companion, my only escape. Greasy burgers and fries turned into glazed doughnuts and bear claws. I no longer sugar-coated my delinquency, choosing to wolf down as much garbage in front of Mom as I possibly could; the insubordinate animal inside me waiting for her to attack. But she never did.

Never in my life would I pull such a stunt in front of Mac, but then again, he wasn't the one who abandoned me. I wanted her to hurt as much as I did, but couldn't even get a rise out of her. Instead I got the "You know Lily, binge eating is generally followed by feelings of guilt and depression. It is a vicious cycle that can lead to long-term side effects that can affect your health negatively. If something is bothering you, we should get to the root of the problem," speech she would give to any one of her patients. Bottom line, she was absolutely clueless and in my eyes, that translated to she didn't care.

Don't get me wrong, I was still upset about her choice to stay at Revitalize rather than coming home with me, but I no longer clung to her side refusing to go home without her. I'm more than sure Mac was grateful for this revelation, seeing as he no longer had to drag me home kicking and screaming.

I too was happy for the change in going-home plans. Now that I was older I had the freedom to linger about. My home away from home became the Salvation Army thrift shop. That's where I splurged on a fifteen-dollar portable DVD player using some of the money I earned from working weekends at Revitalize.

At night, I would pop in videos that I had rented from the library and watch quietly in the comfort of my own bed while Mac slept in his room down the hall. One evening as I reached past the collection of used books cluttering the top of my nightstand to turn off my lamp, it became all too clear. These stories would never desert me. Fantasy became my oasis.

I yearned for an escape. Questioning death, fantasizing about far-off lands – anything that would put an end to my lonely existence. And then one day it came to me. Not by choice, I may add, but it came to me all the same. It all started after draining an electric blue drink (that I should not have had) at THE REAL McKEY, a bar (I should not have been in!).

The day before was a normal one for me. I woke as I always do, shrouded by a black cloud – too depressed to climb out of bed. By eleven o'clock I had arrived at work then was rolled over, once again, by the wheels of my mother's crazy train.

Every hour on the hour I had to walk away from my post at the front desk to visit her up in her suite. This way Orvah could see that I was alive and well. The voices inside her head were giving her the notion that I was in grave danger and although it was a burden to check in, I was happy to prove her wrong time and time again.

Later that night on my way home I saw these two guys watching me. I could have sworn they were following me but it was all a huge misunderstanding thanks to the paranoia planted by my mother's evil seed. Turned out they were just looking for some lost dog, or so I thought at the time.

Anyway, what made the situation worse that day at work was that my co-worker and best friend Sonny was acting peculiar. Normally she was my savior when I was down in the dumps but her behavior only intensified my feelings that day. It was Sonny who suggested we go out for a drink knowing full well that I am under age. God only knows why I agreed but part of it was her nagging and persistent tendencies. Sometimes it's just easier to bite the bullet.

My sanity was already questionable the night we went for drinks. Then after consuming my first alcoholic beverage I could have sworn I was hallucinating. Sonny led me down a deserted hallway at the back of the bar then shape-shifted right before my eyes into one of the men I had seen following me the day before! I was buzz drunk with clouded vision, yet I could clearly see the second man with the aquamarine eyes running toward me. I could sense that I was in trouble. My gut told me to get out of there, but it was impossible – he was blocking my exit. I tried to fight past, but the second he tackled me I felt a burning sensation rip through my body. Shortly after that I lost consciousness.

To my surprise, I woke up in a luxurious meadow surrounded by wildflowers on the edge of a lake. And when my eyes saw a strange man wading in the water under the moonlight I felt, for the first time, a sense of belonging.

I was not delirious. I no longer had to fantasize. The mysterious man with the aqua eyes and the shape-shifting boy with the blonde hair teleported me to a new world. A dimension of Earth where humans possess supernatural powers and mythological creatures roam the land. There in that meadow is where my adventure truly began....

And here on this cliff is where I assumed it would end. After meeting my half-brother Dmitry and joining his quest to rescue our father, the man who had been imprisoned here in Realm since that cold crisp night of March 25, 1992, when he vanished from Patterson Park.

Chapter Three
Mystified

The joy of my father's freedom came crashing down along with the bars that held him. After he crossed over the threshold of the iron prison a seismic vibration caused the cage to crumble and the stone statue to take flight into the night along with a large flock of gulls.

"I thought we were done - I thought this was over," I had cried out.

Now here we are, seconds later, stranded on this deserted island with no place to run or hide as twelve black smoky shadows whiz toward us through the darkening sky. The twelve of us huddle together, waiting in anticipation for what is next to come.

"No, my darling. It's only just begun!" My father had replied.

Whatever it is that's just begun, the team appears to be ready. My aunts Naomi and Nasya concealed themselves within a heavy cloak during the shockwaves first tremor. Dmitry, along with Winston and Warwick (twin brothers from a tribe of land movers) encircle my father, Jaasin, ready to protect him at all costs.

The next thing I know, my brother's best friend Tracy has his arms around me. "No matter what happens, I'll protect you," he whispers into my ear.

The way Tracy's muscular arms grip my waist and the way his warm skin presses against mine, I know he is accountable. To what extent, it doesn't matter. What matters is that I trust him. He has already saved me once before. There was no denying, in the passion of his kiss afterward, that he would do it again.

"I know," I reply before a second set of hands grab me.

My heart skips a beat assuming they belong to Blaze, the first person I met here in Realm. Bathing under the moonlight, his mere presence set my soul on fire. And when he pulled himself from the water revealing that he was a centaur my ad-miration only grew stronger. He took me in, befriended me and accompanied me on this journey.

But when I look up to him, I see he is beyond my reach. Standing at the far end of the crowd, next to Dmitry, he holds Poppy (my brother's girlfriend) tight to his chest. Still weak-ened from her stab to the back, I know all too well he has ap-pointed himself as her guardian. Especially now in the path of the unknown.

The second set of hands turns out to be Alia's, the young-est of our crew, and Poppy's little sister. I feel her soft fragile grasp for only a minute before she lets go, disappearing into thin air.

What I have come to know is that up until a few days ago Alia hadn't spoken in about twelve years. She also showed no signs of having a supernatural ability, like the rest of us have, until today.

Since the moment Tracy, Dmitry and I were trapped in the Chirachnophagous-infested waters she has moved objects with her mind, caused pain, painted a target on Kirill's forehead with the touch of her finger, then took control over the traitor's body. Now, after touching me, she has absorbed my ability and has vanished into thin air.

"Alia, No!" Tracy yells but there is no response. No telling if she is either here or there.

The black clouds of mist glide to the ground solidifying into twelve burly men who instantly surround us.

"Having a party, are we?" the largest of the group asks.

"Don't recall inviting you!" Tracy sarcastically remarks.

"No – but I suppose you know who did – don't you, pretty boy?"

"Leave the child out of this," my father demands from within his cocoon.

"Child?" Tracy grumbles.

"Well if it isn't the man of the hour himself! Alive in the flesh and blood...."

The man takes two steps closer before adding, "But not for long!"

"What's that supposed to mean?"

"Jaasin, Jaasin, Jaasin – I think you know full well what that means."

"Empty threats don't scare me."

"Who said it was empty?"

"Theothantanos has had many opportunities over the years. I'm sure if it was to be done, it would have happened by now."

"Who said anything about the King?"

"Tearlach!" The second largest man cries, "We have our orders – nothing more, nothing less."

"Yes, Vilhelm," Tearlach replies, scowling and bowing slightly to Vilhelm before turning back toward my father. "It took nineteen years, seven accomplices and a mule for you to break free, now did it?"

Blaze's nostrils flair and his jaw clenches with the insult.

"I am not an accomplice!" Kirill's raspy voice quickly interjects.

Tearlach raises an eyebrow, "No?"

Turning to Vilhelm he continues, "The fat one says he's not an accomplice!"

"Then what is he?" Vilhelm questions.

"Your ally!" Kirill responds.

"Why are you speaking?" Tracy growls to Kirill through gritted teeth.

It's not a rhetorical question. Tracy knows full well Alia has had a hold on Kirill since the three of us were rescued from the frozen water. The real question is why doesn't she now?

"Because I can!" Kirill growls back with an evil smirk upon his face.

"MY ally you say?" Tearlach sarcastically remarks.

"The King's, I mean. I knew of their plan to free this piece of filth," (Kirill glances at Jaasin then back to Tearlach), "and followed them. I had all intentions of turning them in but they killed two of my associates on the golden island over there and have been holding me hostage since."

Tracy's muscles tighten. I can feel his anger swell but if he punches Kirill to shut him up it will only confirm he is in fact our foe. Instead he uses great strength and careful wording to shut our friend up.

"Back stabber!" Tracy hisses, hopefully planting a seed.

Tearlach chuckles. "What do you think about all this, Vilhelm?"

"I think – that I am always amazed by how quickly we turn on one another in order to save our own skin."

"No! That is not what I am doing. My name is Kirill Borovsky and I am a tracker. They paid me to find this man so they could free him! I have nothing to do with this!"

"That target tattoo is not the only thing wrong with your head if you believe that." Vilhelm interrupts. "You've got everything to do with this! You just said so yourself."

"No! That is not what I meant."

"You said they paid you to find this felon, did you not?"

"Yes."

"So, you helped them."

"No."

"So, you're telling me that they paid you but you didn't give them the location?"

"Yes! – no, that...."

Vilhelm turns to Tearlach, cutting Kirill off. "See what I mean, this idiot is talking in circles."

"Please, please!" Kirill begs, "check the golden island. Find the bodies of Boris and Christov. I speak nothing but the truth!"

"So help you god," Tearlach grumbles.

And that is it. Kirill snaps his mouth shut knowing he can try to roll over on us as much as he would like, but nothing he says or does is going to change the way he is viewed by Tearlach and his gang. A lying, double-crossing snitch! Thank you, Tracy.

Tearlach looks at each and every one of us before he

speaks again. "And what about the pale little princess? What's her story - eh?"

Okay, I'll give him credit for knowing more words than yabba-dabba-doo, but this caveman has some nerve to poke fun at me. After all he's got the squarest of heads I have ever seen! Literally, like his mother never rolled him over as a baby. I can picture him just lying there like a bump on a log, his soft cranium congealing to the dirt floor.

There is no need to say I'm more than insulted with Fred Flintstone's comment. I mean in Realm, of all places! I never imagined I would be the one being provoked here. Take a good look around. There are Cyclops, Minotaurs, Satyrs, Centaurs (not that there is anything wrong with Centaurs) but still, a much bigger eye-opener than my lack of pigmentation. And what about Vampires? Dollars to doughnuts this oaf has seen one or two at some point in is lifetime. Surely our complexions can't be too far off.

No wonder Naomi and Nasya chose to hide under their cloak. With two heads on top of one body they probably didn't want to be teased about their deformity. And as usual when my mind begins to drift, as it is now, I am reminded of the time when Blaze and I happily strolled through the library. It was just a few days ago yet it somehow feels like a lifetime has passed since that day.

Blaze explained to me the King's prejudices and his quest to create a blemish-free society. How anyone abnormal, disfigured or even as simple as lacking a supernatural ability are banished to a separate expanse of land. Entrapped on an island, never again free to explore the world surrounding them.

Blaze continued to explain that "Hybrids" such as his own kind as well as Minotaurs and Satyrs (the list goes on), surprisingly enough, were considered normal in the King's eyes. Each species collectively has its own duties to fulfill for the monarchy. Centaurs, for example, were amongst those made to serve and protect the King, his castle and the royal grounds. It was Blaze's choice to join the discriminated; for he felt it was the only way he could support them. Refusing his assignments, he joined a crew and set sail for the melting pot, otherwise known as North America on Earth.

And now I'm beginning to worry that the reason this Tearlach questions me is because he wants to ship me off to said continent. All because of the color of my skin? You know that saying, "right church, wrong pew?" Well, try right continent, wrong dimension! Yet in all honesty, it wouldn't be so bad. I could spend my days at the library or picking flowers from the meadow. Swim in the lake under the moonlight with Blaze at my side. Then again, my chances of ever going home would probably be diminished. And if I really want to be honest about this whole scenario the chances of us all getting off scot-free after helping a convicted felon escape are zero to none.

I'm obsessing about all this and scared to death at the same time. Now normally I wouldn't say anything, but really enough is enough and I will have to face whatever consequence comes my way. I've got to start standing up for myself and I figure there's no time like the present. As I draw in a deep breath, summoning up the courage to tell this Neanderthal where to stick it, Tracy squeezes me so tight I almost choke.

"She has fallen ill," Jaasin replies.

Tearlach takes two more steps closer to Poppy and I realize he wasn't referring to me after all. OOPS! I know - cart before the horse every time!

Tearlach reaches out his hand to stroke Poppy's face but his arm stops mid-air. We all watch as he wrestles to move it then snaps it back toward himself with a slight wince.

"Don't you dare touch her!" Dmitry yells, stepping between Blaze, Poppy and Tearlach.

"Was that you?" he asks, looking Dmitry square in the face. Dmitry purses his lips, allowing the silence to speak his mind. Tearlach smiles and again raises his hand.

"Point it at her again and I will break it off!" Dmitry growls.

"Will you now? Eight and a donkey against twelve – Do I

look frightened?"

Things aren't adding up, for the second time this goon has only mentioned eight people when there are actually twelve of us. Well, really eleven if you consider that he isn't aware of Naomi and Nasya's little secret, ten if you categorize Blaze as a horse, donkey, mule... (which he did), nine because Alia has long since disappeared. Eight would mean – ahh ... I was no longer visible as well. I'll hand it to Tracy for the punch to the gut. Best to keep my mouth shut. At this rate, Dmitry should too!

"Frightened or not, I said don't touch her!"

Tearlach grins before his reply.

"As much as I enjoy tormenting you, little fella, I have bigger fish to fry."

Tearlach takes two steps to his right, bringing him face to face with my father. Dmitry follows, taking two steps to his left, causing Tearlach and the eleven other men to chortle.

"Ha, ha, ha, ha, ha! You really think you're going to stop me now, do you?"

"Bet your ass I will!" Dmitry grunts through gritted teeth.

"Let's see it," Tearlach taunts.

Dmitry disappears into a full sprint, kicking up dust in his wake. Super speed being his ability, he comes to an abrupt halt behind Tearlach within seconds. Before any of the King's hired muscle can move, Dmitry has his arms locked around Tearlach's massive neck.

"If you move a single muscle, I'll squeeze." Dmitry murmurs.

Tearlach chuckles once more. His crew joins in, clearly amused by Dmitry's challenge, then poof! Both he and Dmitry vanish.

"No!" Poppy faintly shrieks.

"Shhh, not to worry - he will be back," Blaze consoles.

"You don't know that. He could have teleported Dmitry anywhere. What if...."

Poof!

Tearlach and Dmitry slice through thin air, cutting Poppy

off.

Landing in the same exact spot with Dmitry still clinging to his back, Tearlach barks, "I don't need to blink an eye in order to drag your sorry behind to the ends of the earth and back." He then proceeds to bend forward.

"Nice try though!" He grunts while thrusting Dmitry onto the ground. The sheer force of his action propels Dmitry to the hardened earth with a sickening thud.

"Dmitry!" Poppy cries.

"It's okay. I'm okay," Dmitry assures while picking himself up and dusting himself off. The gashes on his cheekbone and inside corner of his lip speak otherwise.

My father wobbles forward, weak in body, strong at heart.

"If it is me you want, it is me you shall have. All I ask is that you leave them... "

"FATHER, NO!" Dmitry bellows into the evening air.

A blanket of eerie silence descends over us all, causing everyone and everything to fall still. Not a sniffle of a nose, shuffle of a foot, or the whisper of the wind can be heard. It is in this hush that I watch my father's shoulders slump. See the bewildered look on his weathered face as his head shakes disappointingly back and forth. Dread and sorrow brimming in his tired eyes, he speaks. His voice is but a grieving whisper.

"My son, what have you done?"

Chapter Four
Back in Time

"Father?" Tearlach questions. His eyes twinkle with glee. A wide mischievous smile spreads across his face, exposing the large gap between his teeth. "You've never mentioned anything about having a son."

Dmitry's chin nearly hits the ground. I hate times like this, when let's say – inappropriate words just slip out, rolling off your tongue without warning. Dmitry opens and closes his mouth repeatedly like a suffocating goldfish, yet nothing else will follow. It's too late, what's done is done. You can't really retract a statement like that. Not in front of these goons anyway.

"Ah, hah, hah, ha – ha! Who's the jackass now?" Tearlach gloats, glaring at Dmitry with a most satisfied expression before continuing. "Boy, you are just the gift that keeps on giving – aren't ya?"

Tearlach looks over to his minions and nods. Eleven grimacing men signal their comprehension in unison then slowly pad toward us, one plodding step at a time.

Any chance of them just taking Jaasin and leaving the rest of us alone is now null and void. Tracy begins to pull me closer to Dmitry and the others until we are all practically on top of one another. Sardines in a can! Cornered doesn't even begin to describe our current predicament. Dmitry just offered up a fresh bit of news the King must not have known about and I'm sensing we are all in deep doo-doo right about now.

My father holds out his hands, reminding me of the time I took a trip with Orvah on a Greyhound bus to Lancaster County in Pennsylvania. She wanted to show me how the Amish people live. (Which I quickly deduced as being way worse than my family's quirky lifestyle, but that's beside the point.) On the way there, there was an accident on the highway. The driver slammed on his brakes causing the bus to screech to an abrupt halt. My mother's arm dashed out across my chest like a bionic

REALM: RULER OF THE PEOPLE, GOD OF DEATH

seatbelt. This is the same instinctive motion my father is using to protect us now.

"Don't let them touch you. Don't let them touch you!" He murmurs repeatedly. "Not a single finger – Don't let them touch you!"

"NOW!" Tearlach shouts.

All twelve of the King's henchmen spring forward, arms outstretched – hands at the ready. Then bloop! A large iridescent bubble manifests around us and the hirelings bounce back a foot or two.

Tearlach's expression shifts. "I've had enough fun and games for one day!" In a fury he charges forward to pop our bubble. But the second he moves so do we, rising a good ten feet off the ground. Tearlach misses making contact and flies through the air, taking out two of his own companions.

"Damn you!" he roars. "Seize them!"

My heart pounds as I watch each man spiral into large black-clouded mist once more. They dart through the air with intense speed. An icy cold wind rattles through my hair, prickling the back of my skull as I begin to feel a sensation I have experienced only one other time in my life.

A vortex of darkness. Frigid air followed by extreme heat and pressure. It was the REAL McKEY all over again. The last time this happened it was Dmitry forcing me through a portal into Realm. Now, God only knows.

The wind howls so ferociously it's as if several trains were barreling past. Through the pandemonium I can hear faint murmurs from the others, but who it is I cannot say - it's too hard to make out.

"Why are you doing this?" someone asks.

"I'm not!" another responds.

The intense compression feels like I'm being squeezed through a keyhole. Unwittingly I scream. My own voice joins the chaotic buzz, followed by Tracy yelling in my ear.

"I'll never let you go, Lily – I'll never let you go!"

And somehow amidst the entire earsplitting clamor, a

distinctive voice calls out.

"When I get my hands on you I'll ring your pathetic little necks! You hear me? When I find you, and I will - I'll squeeze the life right out of each and every one of you!"

With a fierce CRACK the overwhelming reverberation is replaced with peaceful tranquility. Weightlessness takes over and my body feels free once more. Tracy's death grip squeeze is now a soft caressing hold. His chin nuzzles the inside of my neck and I breathe easy knowing he too feels at ease.

But why?

Why do I have a sense of calm serenity right now? I ask myself. *When we've just been captured and teleported into the house of our enemy?*

I shudder to think what is in store for my family once the King gets his hands on us. Those eyes. The ones I saw glaring down upon me from the banner at the library. Eyes so intense, light gold in color yet so dark. Nothing good would come from our arrest, that's for sure.

I've read all about King Henry VIII. I know what happens to people who commit treason. Instinctively my hand reaches up to touch my neck. I feel the damp precipitation on my tepid skin and swallow hard.

"Why have you brought us here?" Dmitry asks.

Poppy gasps. "I...I..." She whimpers.

"I don't understand." Dmitry states.

"Poppy?" Tracy questions.

I am dying to know what is going on, yet scared to face the truth. Slowly I pull my hands away from my neck and open my eyes, hoping to find the answers to all my questions. Though the vision before me is clear, our reason for being here is foggy. Foggy indeed.

Our bubble hovers a good ten feet over a dried-up field in the center of a large farm. Through the semi-darkened sky I can see two or three scrawny cows mulling about, searching for anything edible to graze on. Another lies dying on the dirt ground, lifting its head occasionally to bellow out a faint moan.

Beyond the animals is a dilapidated farmhouse. Its second story roof had completely caved in at some point in time leaving the tattered chimney standing alone. A large barn is to our right. Its doors are long gone and there are multiple gaps in the siding allowing anyone or anything to walk clear through. And somehow in the midst of all the ruin a few smaller outbuildings stand strong and proud.

Before our bubble descends on the lawn and pops, I scour every inch of the grounds and see we are the only ones present. I have a whole new batch of questions bubbling to the surface. *Where have the King's men gone? How did we get here? And most of all….*

"Where are we?" I burst out. I just have to ask. Answers were not presenting themselves and I was growing tired with the fact that I was unseen and unheard, and my mind was unclear.

Tracy pulls his left hand up from my waist to the top of my shoulder where it pauses momentarily as he moves to the left of me. His hand then moves up and around the nape of my neck to the front of my face where he gently nudges my chin toward his. Catching my cheek with his right hand he pulls my face into his. The way he looks into my eyes tells me I am once again visible.

"We are at the Kruger/Meyer farm," he answers.

"And that is?"

"My farm – my parent's farm," Poppy hesitantly croaks. Tears run down her drawn face.

"Poppy, it's alright," Dmitry consoles.

I can't tell if this is good crying or bad crying so I leave it alone. Poppy swallows hard and nods. I watch intently as Dmitry waits for her to take a few deep breaths before speaking to her again.

"My love…."

He strokes her hair. "Why have you brought us here?"

"I didn't"

"Then how did we get here – and why?"

"I don't know," she replies. "It wasn't me. You know that! I can only push the bubble." She cries, her eyes reddening up.

"But the bubble."

"Forget the bubble. I didn't do it. I don't have the strength."

Poppy has the ability to create bubbles, yet she insists she didn't make this one. Dmitry continues to look longingly into her watery eyes for answers.

"Don't look at me like that," Poppy pleads.

His gaze changes to a more perplexed look.

"I don't understand."

"We teleported!" she whines.

"I know we teleported Poppy, but how? If Tearlach is responsible where in the hell is he?"

Poppy bursts out crying. "The King did this."

"Poppy no, it can't be."

"He is the one who spoiled this land. He is the one who destroyed my family. He is the one tormenting me right now!" she bellows. Her tone dances between deep sorrow and extreme rage.

"He couldn't possibly have connected you to my father. How would he know?"

"He has his ways. He ALWAYS has his ways!" she snaps, pushing her way out of Blaze's arms. Poppy's legs slide to the ground, where she staggers. Blaze helps her by gently holding onto her small frame as she wobbles back and forth, struggling to get her footing. I can't help but think of Bambi right now and the way his knobby knees quivered and trembled to support his weight the first time he stood up. The way he slid and stumbled on ice. I watch as Blaze loosens his grip every so often until Poppy is able to support herself once more.

Hot under the collar, she huffs around in circles searching for the source of our travel, yelling into the air, "You can come out now! I'm not afraid of you! THIS – TIME - MEANS – WAR! DO YOU HEAR ME THEOTHANTANOS?"

"The King didn't bring you here!" A voice echoes from

within the farmhouse.

Poppy spins around so fast she nearly falls to the ground. "Oh no?" she barks, her hazel eyes dilating. "Then who did?"

"I did!" the confident voice replies.

Chapter Five
Blackout

"Who said that?" Poppy roars. "Show yourself!"

We all watch in anticipation as a small shadow steps into the doorway.

"Alia?" Poppy whispers.

She has changed out of her old ripped clothing into a fresh pair of faded-out jeans and a baggy white peasant top. The slightly oversized attire makes her look younger and smaller than she had looked just hours before. Alia's tawny hair is now tied back off her face and she has a large rucksack packed to the gills hanging off her left shoulder. Quickly she strides over to the group.

"It's the only place that came to mind," she says matter-of-factly. Her tone is as brisk as her movements. Kissing Poppy on the cheek, she tosses the bag into Tracy's arms and continues. "We need supplies and I didn't want to lead them to our house."

"But this IS our home," Poppy adds.

"No Poppy, this WAS our HOUSE. I lived here for twelve years, nine of them being a constant source of emotional distress until you agreed to move in with Dmitry, Naomi, Nasya and Tracy."

She pauses to look at Tracy.

"They saved me. They gave me life. The cottage is our home. It is where my heart is...."

She returns her gaze to Poppy. "This, this is the past and that is exactly where it is going to stay!"

Poppy looks as if she just sucked on a sour lemon. She clearly disagrees with Alia, yet doesn't interject.

"I assume it won't be long before they find us here, if they're not already on their way."

Alia stops, takes out a piece of parchment, closes her eyes and takes a deep breath. After a moment's pause a map begins to stir. Fifteen dots appear. She moans slightly then adds. "Yes, any minute. Huddle up! I've got one more bag to get. Oh...."

She looks at Blaze before adding, "And grab that heifer. She'll soon pass and we'll need something to eat."

Alia darts into the house, leaving Blaze with a disgusted look on his face. After a moment's pause in which he doesn't do as Alia had asked, Winston and Warwick walk over to the passing cow and gently lift her into their arms.

Tools and, or weapons, (whichever way you want to look at it), food, clothing and pretty much everything but the partridge and the pear tree are loaded into our bubble. Alia lifts us into the air and stops. Suspended in the middle of the farm we bob up and down like a buoy in the sea.

"Now what?" Dmitry asks.

"Precisely," Alia agrees. Again, she touches the paper and closes her eyes. Only two dots remain on the map. "They have a tracker. They know we are here."

"Then they will always know where we are," Dmitry states.

"Not necessarily," Kirill offers.

Alia's eyes open, looking intently at Kirill.

"Where?"

"Aravalli Range."

And before anything else is said, before anyone can object, I feel the familiar tugging sensation behind my navel and know within seconds a ton of pressure is going to be unleashed against my tiny frame and squeeze me once again into oblivion.

Images swirl before me as I enter the vortex of darkness. Black billowing figures manifesting into eleven men. I hear a loud noise but it isn't the familiar roar of a train. It is a sharp snap, like that of a large limb separating from its tree. Then I hear smaller cracking pops that sound like the limb is splintering to the ground, followed by the almighty thud of it making contact with the earth. I can see the large bark-covered trunk, a gnarled root at its end.

They have found us. They have found us indeed! This

time I feel the extreme heat first. So hot I can almost see the flame. Then comes the frigid air. Air so cold it fills my lungs with ice every time I take a breath. It pulls me into the darkness, consuming me, trying to turn me into stone.

The next thing I know my body is tumbling to the ground. I roll onto an icy cold summit surrounded by large chunks of frozen rock. Dmitry topples on top of me, Winston and Warwick to my side. It's as if the twelve of us are ice cubes, shaken into a snow-capped mountain martini glass.

Poppy with her torn shirt, Tracy's bare chest, my jeans that have been shredded into shorts with the barely-there tank top I have on. We are all in danger of freezing to death. My skin is so cold I want to cry out but the thin air at this altitude is making it near impossible for me to breathe, let alone scream. My head pounds as I feel my body shutting down. Frostbite is already setting in.

Kirill! I think to myself. He must have known we wouldn't survive the harsh weather conditions and lured us to this ice-covered peak under false pretenses in order to kill us once and for all. But if that was the case, how does he intend to survive? Surely his blubber and greasy trench coat aren't enough insulation to get him down the mountain. I highly doubt his girth will allow him to even navigate the rugged terrain to a milder climate.

I stare at him wondering what could be going through his thick skull when he wheezes, "Wrong mountain, you stupid girl!"

So, this wasn't his plan after all? I must not be the only one to accuse Kirill of deception because all heads turn from him to Alia, awaiting an answer. I can see her hot breath rolling off the tip of her tongue out into the crisp air, forming the words she mutters ever so quickly.

"And for good reason, you fool."

Her eyes pull away from Kirill. She looks at Dmitry then glares from Tracy to Winston, then Warwick and finally Blaze. "We don't have a lot of time," she confirms. The five men nod in agreement.

And it doesn't take long for the next series of events to unfold. I struggle to get a footing, stumbling repeatedly as I try to pull myself up off the snow that has already adhered to my skin. Tiny pieces of flesh tear free from my arms and knees as I begin to stand, causing me great pain. Especially since both my arms and legs are already scraped and torn from climbing up the rocks to my father's cage.

Everything is happening so fast my mind can't make heads or tails of what is going on. But one thing is certain and that is how quickly I'm heading downhill.

I'm telling myself to move, yet all I can muster are a few awkward spasms in between the violent shivering and convulsing my body is doing at the moment. Tracy grabs me and I am thankful for his help until I see the look on his face. Hastily he shoves me back to the ground between a set of large boulders. His actions are harsh and I am taken aback by his hostility.

My mind instantly creates a madcap notion in which Tracy understands the severity of our situation, knows my body is shutting down and therefore is going to put an end to my misery. After all, why should I suffer a slow death? The thought both comforts and terrifies me all the same.

"Do NOT disappear!" he demands.

"I, I ty not to," I gurgle. The sound of my own voice startles me. It's a combination of trying not to cry while forcing myself to speak, which is hard because all my body wants to do is shake. Lacking control, fright sets in and tears bubble forth, freezing to my eyes, crusting my lashes. Icicles of snot form around my nose and the worst part of me begins to think what a pitiful sight I must be.

"Don't go anywhere, I mean it!" he shouts.

I want nothing more than to yell back. *I can't! I can't even talk, let alone fade!* Which is kind of ironic because that is exactly what I am doing. Fading away. The demented idea of Tracy wanting to be able to see me when he does me in takes over. How else could he bash me over the head or something like that?

Lord of the Flies. I shudder to think but the only words that come out of my mouth are, "I – do." I mean what is wrong with me?

The least Tracy could do is transform into something or someone else so it's not so bad. Trick my mind into thinking I was about to be trampled to death by an elephant or eaten by a mountain lion rather than being brutally attacked by a man who I thought loves me. Well maybe love is stretching it! More like really, really likes me.

But wait! I still have a second chance for survival. Blaze! I gaze to him – his arrow is drawn. I gulp in horror. A piercing sensation hits my chest and a flame begins to flicker within me. My body stops shivering and for the first time since we landed here I feel warmth. Hot instant relief - thank you Blaze. The man, not his arrow, who sets my soul on fire.

I am officially going crazy. First I find myself freezing, which hurts so much part of me aches, wishing for death. The rational part of me knows Tracy would never hurt me. Then I see that Blaze's arrow is still drawn and pointing in the opposite direction.

A surge of heat flickers to the surface as my body tells me one thing and my mind is telling me another. Hypothermia! I have all the classic signs, the shivering, stumbling, mental confusion and difficulty speaking. Now the part of my brain that regulates body temperature is malfunctioning and I believe myself to be warm once more.

I still can't talk or walk. My body shakes even though I am burning right now, telling me it is the end. I can slip forth from this life feeling warm and free yet I don't want to. I'm not ready!

You'd think I'd be used to this by now. My life has been threatened and I've come close to death several times since I arrived here in Realm. You'd think I would be able to start the Paradoxil Undressing and raise my hands in the air. Lily Monroe, her own little white flag! But I can't. I don't have the energy for movement or speech. Vision is the only thing I have left.

I watch as Dmitry throws my father into my frozen arms and Tracy forces Poppy to the right of me. After that Winston guides Nasya and Naomi to my left up against the rock formations while Kirill, cowardly, backs himself into a corner.

Through the array of angry determined eyes - Alia – Tracy – Dmitry – Blaze – Winston – Warwick - I see it.

Black night. White ice. Red fire. Tree trunk.

Only, it's not a tree trunk after all!

BLAZE

Chapter Six
Intuition

Sometimes I wonder what I have signed myself up for. I loved my quiet life back home in the woods. I know other expanses of land have just as many ideal locations for the perfect house but relocating to the Melting Pot was one of the best decisions I could have made. It was a great way to support the discriminated but also proved to be the most tranquil place in Realm.

For what most don't understand when they are forced into exile is how lucky they truly are. Once you have arrived, there is no persecution, no hostility and no more judgment. You will never again experience someone looking down his or her nose at you, for everyone in the Melting Pot is equal.

Its population is a perfect blend of life in all of its forms, which is magnificently beautiful and should be cherished.

Now don't get me wrong, not everyone agrees. Not everyone who is sent to the Melting Pot feels as I do. There is and always will be a small percentage of those who try to break free. Usually right after placement because they are in denial. Homesick, missing loved ones or downright resentful. Blinded by emotions, they take to the sea.

They should know better. There is no escape. My heart aches for their light, extinguished by those who work to keep us there. Their bodies are swept away in a crimson tide, their souls lost forever.

Aerosaurs! True secrets amongst our society. Introduced to me the day Dmitry came for Lily. Magnificent, camouflaged flying creatures that tell me there is so much more to learn in this world.

There is an old saying; "You learn something new every

day." I believe in this motto. Keeping an open heart and mind unlocks a gateway to maximum comprehension. It is one hundred percent true - if you are willing, that is.

Having a thirst for knowledge, I have read about Scylla and Charybdis. I listened to the myths surrounding them, but never in my wildest dreams did I ever imagine seeing such vile creatures. Nor did I envision coming face to face with a Hecatonchires. But a noble man always protects his family and that is exactly what Lily Monroe is to me now.

Her aura at the side of the lake that night was overwhelming. When she finally showed herself to me I thought for sure heaven had dropped an angel. Instantly smitten, I promised myself to keep her safe until she was back home on Earth.

I found her alone, scared and extremely green. Like the flower she is named after, she blossoms. Unsure, unaware ... but she is so much more.

I didn't like the sight and smell of those two the moment they ambushed us in the library. Dmitry and Tracy – Tracy and Dmitry. Two rowdy delinquents on some harebrained mission to save Dmitry's father! Carelessly forcing Lily through a barrier into our dimension, trying to convince her she is family.

At first I didn't like Dmitry's daring approach or Tracy's lascivious behavior and the fact that they had us surrounded.

Blood proved thicker than water when Lily opted to join them with no proof other than her gut feelings. Intuition – the ability to understand something immediately without the need for conscious reasoning. I smiled in that moment, knowing she was a force to be reckoned with.

Still I had no intentions of having her go at it alone with a group of strangers, even though I could smell a familial match. At first there was no trusting them. Lily is delicate and this is a new world for her. A world that has threatened her precious life time and time again since the moment she stepped foot in it. A world that has introduced her to her father but also encased her within a frozen tomb, leaving her to drown or be ravaged by sea monsters. It is a world that I will not let take her, as it is trying to do once again, so I will continue to fight.

Even though I wonder what I have signed myself up for I am grateful to have joined this expedition. Through this short endeavor I have grown accustomed to the group. Dmitry is a committed gentleman. Tracy, though coquettish, is loyal and strong. Naomi and Nasya are nurturing, Poppy is frisky, Winston and Warwick are true saviors, and the little one - well, she is strikingly bold.

My instinct is to trust Alia, as I would trust all of them now. When she flashes those umber eyes, intuition takes over. I know full well what she needs us to do, and time is of the essence. We must move quickly and precisely if Lily is going to make it out of here alive. Though she is not the only one I worry about in times like these.

Half our team is delicate. Too fragile to fight, yet we must do right by them. Tracy grabs Lily, hastily shoving her between a set of large boulders. It is not ideal, but it is all time will allow for any kind of concealment.

I detest the way Tracy shouts at her, but every word he speaks is true. Now is not the time for Lily to vanish from sight. The severity of Tracy's tone and the look on her face as she sees my drawn bow and arrow tells me she will do just that. If we succeed we will have to relocate fast. Searching for Lily is not an option.

Jaasin, Poppy, Naomi, Nasya and Kirill have tucked themselves in beside Lily. I am optimistic that their body heat will radiate within the tiny crevice, warming them all, especially Lily who is in a hypothermic state. Still she could leave us all in a split second and that is what I worry about most.

A deafening crack splinters through the air, causing Naomi and Nasya to lock their arms around Lily. Their action gives me the only sense of relief I have amongst the chaos and it is the last reflection my mind will allow me to process about her. For now, every ounce of my attention, every ounce of strength and every thought in my mind must be about battling what has just teleported in front of us.

A charcoal reptilian leg the size of a great white oak slams down on the frozen earth, bouncing chunks of ice and rock against its prickly armor. Sharp scaly toes dig into the mountain, clawing its way toward the six of us.

Alia disappears in a flash, reappearing atop the draconem's back behind two men that are perched between its thorny shoulder blades. Tearlach, the mesomorphic underling who threatened our lives back at the cage, is the one guiding this beast. It is a true testament of his power.

To his surprise, Alia spears him in his back with a small serrated knife, no doubt puncturing his kidney. Tearlach flinches, pulling hard on the reins, causing the monster's head to rise and its nostrils to emit a large cloud of smoke. Tearlach then elbows Alia hard in the chest causing her to fall backwards against the dragon. He turns then dives towards the child. One touch of his hand against her throat and they both vanish from sight.

Eleven swirls of black mist begin to reshape into human form. I spare not a single second before firing off half a dozen arrows, striking six men through the heart, one of them being Vilhelm, Tearlach's deputy. Their limp bodies fall to the ground before the four remaining men have time to complete the transformation.

The remaining man upon the dragon, who I assume to be the tracker, takes over the reins. The beast protests, jerking and wrenching about while the tracker tugs and pulls back with all his might. It then roars in anger, throwing an inferno of fire out into the night sky directly at the rock formations Lily and the rest are hiding behind.

My heart skips a beat as flames lick the boulder but I don't dare react. Tracy on the other hand yells, "NOOOOO!" before spinning into a large funnel cloud at the same time Dmitry sprints up the monster's tail after its rider.

With each twirl Tracy's tornado grows larger and larger until a second dragon emerges. Unlike the first beast, which has more of a Bulgarian look (as those on Earth would describe it) with dark shingles that resemble the bark of a tree, razor-sharp spikes down its spine and bat-like wings, Tracy's dragon has more Asian attributes. He has transformed himself into a crimson red and gold monster with the great horns of a stag and long black whiskers.

Tracy roars in anger, shooting flames out his crocodile mouth toward the steel grey dragon. It yelps in agony then takes to the sky with Dmitry and the tracker fist-fighting one another between the spikes on its back.

In one swoop Tracy turns, forcing more flame out of his mouth, engulfing three of the four remaining guards. He then lunges into the sky after the first giant reptile, taunting it into a duel in the most vexing manner. With a few swipes of his tail and several nips into its scaly armor, Tracy has managed to bring the beast around.

He then takes off up the mountain followed by the charcoal draconem. The sudden shift in direction causes Dmitry to lose his footing and he tumbles into the air, pulling the tracker down with him. At about three thousand feet or more, both Dmitry and the tracker begin a freefall toward the hard rock below. Their bodies separate as they accelerate to terminal velocity. I use this moment to my advantage, taking aim then spearing the tracker through his chest.

That is when I feel my body pull away from me. My flesh becomes numb, my mind fuzzy, and my vision begins to swirl. It feels as if something has me by the tail, tugging me into the midst of a small cyclone. My suspicions are confirmed after I kick my hind legs.

Sprawled out behind me on the icy summit is the last of the King's guards. Too weak to transport my mass, he has only managed to carry us a little farther up the mountain range. The distance he has created between me and the others is unsettling.

Gazing down the ledge I can see the blackened rock formations Lily and the gang are sheltered behind. Winston and Warwick standing at their edge, waiting for their cue. I spy

Dmitry still falling toward the snowy ground where Alia and Tearlach have just appeared, and the two dragons still racing through the sky.

The air at this altitude is thin and I can hear the minion's rattled breath before he touches me a second time. Though I can't imagine he has the strength to move us again, I will not risk being any farther away from Lily than I am now.

Watching Tearlach pin Alia to the ground, my muscles tighten. He straddles her then smiles into her adolescent face as he wraps his hands around her petite neck.

"A real man would look his enemy in the eyes, you know," I state, my own eyes never straying from the grisly scene below.

The rattling grows louder as the guard approaches from behind. Cradling his abdomen he steps before me, drained from the kick to the gut and lack of oxygen. Theoretically I could leave him here to die. But I won't take that chance. Not until Lily is safe back home. Anyone who can connect her to Jaasin's escape, anyone who can bring her before the King must be eliminated.

And that is exactly what I do. Eliminate the threat by cervical fracture. His limp body tumbles to the ground, clearing my briefly obstructed view.

Tracy is now soaring through the air toward me. He barrel-rolls over my head then darts down the ice-covered mountain. His yellow belly grazes the ground as he speeds toward Dmitry and Alia. With his opponent heavy on his tail, Tracy tucks his chin and head-butts Tearlach off Alia at the exact moment Dmitry lands safe and sound on his back.

Within a fraction of a second Alia vanishes from the ground. Dmitry springs to life, sprinting down Tracy's back and out of sight. The red dragon circles then lands with a loud thud a good two hundred feet from where Tearlach lies wounded on the ground. Tracy gazes toward me on the mountaintop, raises his neck high into the air, then cries out into the night throwing a set of sparks into the black sky.

The second beast crash-lands on top of Tearlach, instantly crushing the man, then howls back at Tracy, spitting fire. Rocking back on its hind legs the charcoal demon claws at the red dragon.

Tracy takes a nasty blow to the face from its spiked tail then defensively spins into his familiar wind cloud. The typhoon intrigues the other beast and it watches as Tracy rotates around, shrinking in size. The animal's eyes dilate in curiosity. Then like a cat about to strike it crouches down against the ground watching, waiting to pounce.

Now is the perfect time.

The ground begins to quake below my feet and I instinctively take a step back from the crest. Winston and Warwick are moving the earth. When they finish loosening its icy crust, an avalanche of snow thunders down the gully, burying the thorny beast.

Tracy, who has transformed into a firebird, darts into the air just in the nick of time. Soaring high over the fresh blanket of snow, he fills the sky with a magnificent display of red, yellow and gold lights.

Though it is nothing short of spectacular I mustn't waste time getting back to Lily. Before I can take off and descend down the mountain a large bubble is already floating toward me.

"Lily?" I call out the second it greets me on the range.

"We've got her!" Naomi and Nasya respond in unison.

As predicted she has veiled herself once again. What I cannot see of her I feel. Taking her into my arms, her body feels supple and dewy. Relieved, I pull her in to me, cradling her against my tepid skin

"The fire?" I ask.

"The rocks took the brunt of it. What flashed over was high enough to warm our frigid bones," Jaasin croaks.

I nod in understanding.

"Awesome!" Tracy's voice rings out from behind me.

Except for the large gash under his right eye he appears to be back to his old self.

"That went better than I thought it would!" he gloats.

"Good enough," Alia exclaims, inadvertently stroking her neck. "Anyway, we should have enough time to disappear...."

"Lily!" Tracy shouts.

"I've got her," I state.

There is no need for a verbal response when his body language speaks the words. First there is a flare of his nostrils, a quick flash in his eyes followed by the clenching of his jaw. His chest heaves, his shoulders tense, then his mouth opens. With extreme control a sequence of words roll off his tongue.

"Is she alright?"

Again, I nod.

"Fine then," Tracy responds then turns away. Dmitry throws his arm around Tracy, squeezes the top of his shoulder, and praises him with a "Good job!"

I'm not sure of the implication, as it can mean one of three things. Good job for distracting the dragon long enough for Winston and Warwick to bury it alive. Good job for saving my life once again or good job for not wearing your heart on your sleeve. Or it could be the entire lot.

Tracy exhales rather loudly before adding, "Right?" in his usual self-assured egotistical way. Turning to Dmitry, Tracy continues. "Man, you really grew a set back there! Racing up that dragon's spine like you did - I couldn't believe it – I mean you – of all people! What were you thinking?"

"I – I wasn't. Not about the dragon, that's for sure. I was caught up in the moment and wanted...." Dmitry trails off, lost in thought.

"YOU wanted? You know what I want more than anything my friend?" Tracy asks.

"What's that?"

"Is for you to stop dropping out of the sky like that!" Tracy continues.

"I know. I'm just thankful you were there to save my skin, yet again."

"Yeah well, our bromance can't survive without you. But

thrice is more than enough."

"Agreed!"

I'm not sure what a bromance is but I am certain that I have had my fill of listening to Tracy's street talk in the short amount of time it took Alia to teleport us to a new location. This humid grassy row of worn-down mountain is most likely the Aravalli Range our portly traitor spoke about earlier. As the group loiters in front of an underground chamber, Lily begins to stir, as do my senses.

"We can only be concealed within its depths," Kirill states.

But something tells me we shouldn't.

"Don't do it." I direct my words specifically toward Alia and Dmitry.

"Why should we trust you?" Dmitry asks Kirill. Though he can't possibly expect a hardened criminal to be trustworthy in the first place, especially after what he did to Poppy.

"Don't for all I care," Kirill barks. "The choice is yours." Then he makes to cut and run.

"I don't think so!" Alia scolds, stopping Kirill from departing.

"I have told you where to seek solace."

"But that is not all you will find," I interject. "I have a feeling...."

"As do I...." Alia interrupts, "that he will tell the King where to find us." Turning to Kirill she continues, "Once a fink, always a fink! I keep friends close and my enemies even closer, therefore I have no intentions of letting you go," Alia rages.

Headstrong and ignoring any possible danger, she marches Kirill into the cave. Poppy and Jaasin are the next to follow Alia. Winston and Warwick escort Naomi and Nasya through its mouth, causing the hair to rise on the back of my neck.

"I wouldn't do that if I were you," I call in warning. Unmoved by my words they continue, disappearing down into the belly of the cave.

"Dmitry!" I plead.

"Why, Blaze?" Dmitry questions.

"I fear a threat like none other. There is evil down in that – that crypt."

"As there is out here in the open, but if we are to stay out of the King's clutches it is our only chance to go undetected."

"Jaasin is the only one who needs to sequester himself," I declare.

"And I shall leave my father to avoid the King's eye all on his own? I can't! By now Theothantanos will have learned there is a son."

"Then go as well, just you. There is no need to involve the others!"

"Yet they already are involved. This group is a team. One for all and all for one."

"I am warning you, no good can come of this!"

"And no good can come of us staying out here in the open," Dmitry states before turning toward the cavern.

"Dmitry, wait!" Lily calls, stopping him from entering. Dmitry turns to her.

Forcefully she pries herself out of my hold.

"Lily?" both of us question.

"I'm coming with you!"

"No!" I cry, grabbing her arm.

"Dmitry is right. I won't abandon my family."

"But I can't protect you if you choose to enter without me."

"Then come with us," She pleads.

"I can't."

"Can't or won't?"

"Lily, it's not that simple."

"I see!"

"No, you don't see - no one can - but I feel it, trust in me."

"What am I trusting?"

"My instinct. That's all I have to go on."

"What about mine?"

"Lily, don't do this – you mustn't go!"

"What other choice do I have?"

"Stay - with me."

"And leave them all behind?" she questions, giving Dmitry a glance. "He's my brother."

"And I?" I question, backing away from the cave.

"Blaze?" Lily whispers, and I know in the tone of her voice what choice she has made.

"Dmitry, you will regret the decision not to heed my warnings. Lily, my darling, you will too."

"Blaze!"

"Your decision is clear, and all your own. Take with you the knowledge that I swore to protect you the moment I saw your beautiful face by the lake that night. I knew in that moment I would do anything to keep you safe. You are tying me in knots right now and I must go before my emotions get the better of me. Please - forgive my decision – forgive me."

And with that I turn from her.

"NO!" I hear her yelling over and over again. She is calling my name, pleading for me not to go – not to leave her. Her calls are followed by Dmitry's utterance; soothing and calm, assuring her everything will be all right. Both voices disappear the second they step into the cavern, leaving silence in their wake.

Her fear.

My honor.

Her love.

I turn to the cave for a final goodbye. Tracy, leaning against the rock wall, meets my eyes. For the second time he doesn't have to say a thing. I know immediately, without the need for conscious reasoning.

My intuition.

He will take my place.

DMITRY

Chapter Seven
Why?

"Shhhh Lily, don't cry – you don't have to cry," I whisper into her ear.

After I usher her down a dark dank tunnel into a large den where the rest of the group is waiting, Lily curls into my chest.

"It will be alright, I promise."

"None of this is okay," She mumbles.

"What happened? Why is she crying, Dmitry?" Naomi questions. Though I would like to deduce the reasoning behind her tears is because Blaze stayed behind, I can't be so sure. Women are so complex and I am guessing her emotions are as well. Lily's been through so much in the last eighteen hours and it's a lot to take in. My response to Naomi is simple, a shrug of the shoulders.

"Oh, Lily!" Nasya gasps, then runs to Lily, embracing her with loving arms. "Why are you crying?"

"Because Blaze has left the group." Tracy interjects, taking a stand by my side.

"Is this true?" Nasya asks.

Lily nods in confirmation.

"Why?" Naomi wants to know.

"He feels there is an unknown threat in this bunker. His instincts will not allow him to enter," I explain.

"Wouldn't it be wise to hear him out?" Winston questions. "After all he is a hybrid. Part of him will have a much keener sixth sense than you or I."

"We don't have the time, we need this concealment – NOW! Soon the King will realize things have gone awry. When that time comes he will gather new troops, if he hasn't already, and send them out to hunt us down," Alia states.

"Alia is right, we need the cover now more than ever before. My father is not the only one the King will be after at this point."

"Yes, unfortunately he is now aware of your existence, Dmitry, but the real question is, how many trackers could Theothantanos have at his disposal and how many more 'blind spots' exist for us to hide out in?" Winston wonders.

All eyes fall upon Kirill.

"What?" Kirill answers.

"Answer the man!" Alia commands.

"Fine! I possess a very rare talent."

"That we already know. It took us over half a year to find you. Not everyone that possesses your talent renders their services," I add.

"Tell us more," Alia orders.

Kirill hesitates at first then begrudgingly continues with, "At the moment his Majesty does not have a second. He will not be able to track a tracker down in a timely fashion without the use of a tracker."

"She sells seashells on the seashore. The shells she sells are seashells, I'm sure!" Tracy sings.

"Mocking me, are you?" Kirill barks.

"Tracy!" I scold.

"What? I couldn't help it!" Tracy admits.

"I'm sorry for my friend's outburst, please – we need to know more."

"It will take the Sovereign time to find one, but unlike you, the first tracker that he finds will do the job. If you know what I mean?"

"Understood."

"We will have time to move," Winston declares.

"Possibly so," I ponder.

"To where?" Alia cries defensively, clearly angered by the possibility. Raising her voice, she attacks Kirill with more questions. "Well? Where else can we go that doesn't possess an instinctual threat for Blaze?"

"I cannot make any guarantees. I know of no danger here."

"Where ELSE can we go?" she barks.

"I am only aware of one other place."

"But if you know, won't all the other trackers?" I ask.

"It is not common knowledge."

"Then how did you find these blind spots?"

"That is for ME to know!"

"Dmitry, we are wasting precious time. I say we go with Blaze. Unite the group and find a spot he is comfortable with before it is too late," Winston adds.

Being torn between the possibilities, I merely nod my head, neither agreeing nor disagreeing with Winston's suggestion.

"How are we to know Blaze won't have a problem with the second place? Huh? What will we do then?" Alia rages and I have to admit her attack is wearing on me. I find myself getting a little heated when I ask her to calm down.

"Calm down? – CALM DOWN? FOR THE FIRST TIME IN OVER EIGHTEEN HOURS WE ARE SAFE. SAFE TO REST - SAFE FOR MY SISTER TO HEAL - AND NOW YOU WANT TO GO AND RISK EVERYTHING? ENDANGER HER LIFE AGAIN? YOUR SISTER'S? YOUR FATHER'S? WHY? FOR WHAT? I SAY WE'RE STAYING AND THAT IS FINAL!"

That's it!

"YOU SAY? WHO THE HELL DO YOU THINK YOU ARE? THIS IS MY MISSION. IT STARTED WITH MY BEST FRIEND AND ME TO SAVE MY FATHER. YOU HAVE NO RIGHTS TO BOSS US ALL AROUND THE WAY YOU ARE! I HAVEN'T DIED AND LEFT YOU BOSS!"

"IF IT WASN'T FOR ME YOU WOULD BE DEAD!" Alia screams.

"NO! IF IT WEREN'T FOR TRACY, LILY AND I WOULD BE FERMENTING IN THE BELLY OF A CHIRACHNOPHAGOUS RIGHT NOW - AND IF IT WEREN'T FOR BLAZE ALL THREE OF US WOULD HAVE PERISHED UNDER THE ICE!"

Then it hits me. How could I just let him walk away? He

saved my life. Lily – Tracy - Winston and Warwick, he saved us all. Blaze carried Poppy when I was too weak. He ushered us, strangers that he just met, through hard times to free my father. He fought for us and now I owe him restitution for my lack of gratitude. I owe him the sense of security I have fought so hard for for each member of this team except him. I should have followed his intuition but I didn't. How can I be so obtuse time and time again?

"Blaze saved my life, Alia. Not you. We're going after him."

"YOU BASTARD!" she growls. Her face is flushed, her eyes like daggers. I see her tiny fist waiting, ready to strike.

The simple sight of her this way stirs the savage animal within me. I have to hand it to her. It usually takes quite a bit more to set me off. But the words are already rolling off my tongue, regret already sinking in, before my rant is through.

"You best watch your mouth, Alia! You have some nerve calling me obscenities when you are nothing but yourself. A pig-headed git since the day I met you. And from what I gather you have been since the day the King took your mother away when you were nearly three years old. Refusing to talk, refusing to eat. You're nothing but a selfish little girl who throws temper tantrums to get your own way regardless of the consequences to those around you! Manipulating my liberation to do it again. Well, you'd best shut your face 'cause it's not going to work this time."

Alia's hand rises.

"Use your powers, whatever they may be, on any member of this group and god help you – you're as good as gone. Got it missy? 'Cause I'm in charge here and what I say goes! Grab your shit, we're getting out of here."

Alia opens her mouth to strike back but I beat her to the punch with a final blow.

"I liked you better when you didn't talk," I lash out, then walk away. I have no other choice. It was way below the belt and I know I shouldn't have said it. I shouldn't have said any of it. Yet I did, all because I wanted her to shut up, which is precisely what she does.

When I turn back around I see Alia has crouched down to the ground. Her arms are folded over one another, safeguarding her chest and for the first time since we battled Gyes she looks fragile once more.

"Alia, don't," Poppy cries.

Reverting back to her code of silence Alia just shakes her head.

I make myself sick.

"Hey buddy, you alright?" Tracy asks in a consoling manner.

"No."

"Don't beat yourself up. We are all famished and over-tired. We've all said things we regret since the get-go. It's the nature of the beast. I wouldn't want to tell you what to do – since you're the chief of this tribe and all, (he pauses to flash his infamous smile), but we should stay the night. Nosh a little – take a nice long siesta then start over in the morning. You'll have no trouble catching up to Blaze and we'll all be back together with a new plan by nightfall tomorrow. Whadya say?"

Succumbing to fatigue, I merely nod my approval. Tracy's right. I'm not the only one at the end of his rope. We've been through so much; nourishment and rest is essential.

"Okay then. It's settled." Tracy's voice booms to the crew. "First, we are going to get some food in our bellies, followed by some well-deserved sleep. When we awake, Dmitry will find Blaze and we'll all regroup before setting off to our second location." He pauses to glance at Alia, then to Lily and back to me before continuing. "It's the perfect compromise, you know."

Winston and Warwick take over, starting the preparations for our small camp, rifling through rucksacks for pots, pans and silverware. Naomi and Nasya lay out a few blankets while Jaasin focuses his attention on the cow.

After trying to bring Alia around to no avail Poppy rummages for some clean clothes for herself and offers Lily a white eyelet baby doll dress. It's the first time Lily has smiled since we opened the cage that held our father. The thought brings back the memory of my last outburst, which resulted in me slitting my own sister's wrist, and I cringe.

My god what kind of monster am I? I ask myself.

Slowly I walk over to Alia and crouch down beside her. She turns her face away from me – rightfully so.

"I – I am so sorry. There's no excuse for what I said to you." Gently, I place my hand on her leg. Alia neither pulls away nor embraces it. She does not reply verbally but after a minute or two she looks into my eyes and pulls her mouth into a small grimace, which is fine for me. It tells me all is not forgiven but the damage can be repaired in time.

The two of us sit side by side watching Warwick tear the flesh from the recently departed heifer while Winston fries it up in a pan for all of us to eat. Naomi and Nasya are slicing raw potatoes to throw on the fire and Jaasin is placing handfuls of nuts into bowls.

Kirill, who is sitting obediently on Alia's other side, is practically salivating. The thought of feeding him makes me want to go ballistic once again. He nearly killed the love of my life and for all I care he can starve to death, but I think I've proven myself barbaric enough for one day. And Alia is right; he could be useful to us at some point. So, I will let him live - for now.

Poppy and Lily are sitting together opposite me in their fresh clothes, both combing through their tangled hair with the tips of their dainty fingers, which brings a smile to my face. I study Poppy with her torn lip and pale face. Still weak from being stabbed but always a fighter. God, I love that woman so much!

Thank you for not leaving me.

My sister. Just as stubborn, naïve and confused as I. It is amazing how someone you just met can have such a huge impact on your life.

I am so thankful to have found you.

Tracy paces slowly back and forth between us, his eyes stealing glimpses of Lily every chance he has. Quiet and withdrawn, I can see he is not himself - siding against Alia and agreeing to team up with Blaze once more. A staple in Lily's life, a thorn in his own side.

Thank you for being my best friend.

My father, frail and malnourished, happily passes food out to everyone in the group, making darn sure they all have a hearty serving before ladling the remaining scraps into his own bowl. The look on his face after he takes his first bite of warm meat and potato is more than I can bear.

Thank you for coming back to me.

I don't remember falling asleep, or any dream or nightmare that might have danced in my head as I slumbered soundly, tucked up against Poppy's warmth. But waking in the morning is another story. My mind is groggy, my body full of aching muscles. With a groan of displeasure and a dry mouth I force myself to sit up, noticing that Alia and my father are the only other ones awake.

"Did you rest well, my son?"

"Yeah, it's just the waking up part that's not going so good," I yawn in response.

"Come here." He beckons.

Pulling me into his embrace he hugs me tight. The second his hands rub against my back a warm fuzzy sensation emanates from them. It runs up and down my spine sending small pulsating waves throughout my body. In an instant my excruciating pain is relieved thanks to his healing touch.

"Better?" he asks as he releases me.

"Yes. Thank you."

"Oh, don't thank me. I really owe you one and mending sore muscles and small lacerations is about all I can do right now. Speaking of which -"

He then places the palm of his hand against my face,

53

warming my cheek and lip. I feel the rough, dry scab in the corner of my mouth dissolve. Then after he releases me I raise my own hand. Sure enough the tender gash under my eye has dissipated as well.

"Amazing," I marvel.

"Not as much as you," he replies.

"Morning!" Poppy whispers into my ear and I am thankful for the interruption. No matter how pleased I am to have helped Jaasin, he hasn't been my father since I was two and a half years old. That's a little over nineteen years of my life he's missed because he walked out on me. And truth be told, I am still a little sour about it.

"Morning," I reply, kissing her beautiful face. "Did you sleep good?"

"Like a log!"

In the short amount of time since I awoke, Alia has packed up the camp and returned to crouching against the rock wall. Winston, Warwick, Naomi and Nasya are all starting to stir, while Kirill snores obnoxiously loud. I wonder how any of us could have slept through that, how Tracy, who has his arm wrapped around my sister, and Lily are still slumbering through such a ruckus right now.

"What time is it?" Poppy questions.

Taking a good look at my watch, I see twelve hours have passed since we turned in for the night, making it much later than I was hoping it would be.

"Shit! It's past two o'clock in the afternoon! Blaze could be anywhere by now. Come on guys" I yell, rousing the group with the clapping of my hands. "It's late, we've gotta get going!"

Alia jumps to her feet, crosses her arms and shoots me an evil eye before continuing further down the tunnel and out of sight.

"Ah? – Wha?" I groan. I mean what is she doing? The last thing I want to do right now is lock horns again.

"Relax, she'll come around," Poppy comforts.

"I don't know, Poppy, I think I really screwed this one up."

"The truth hurts. It's time for her to grow up and handle things in a more mature way."

"You're not mad at me?"

"For what? Trying to straighten her out? No – Alia is Alia and sometimes she can use a kick in the pants. Come on, let's pack up and go."

"But?"

"She's never been alone a day in her life. She's certainly not going to stay here without us."

"You sure?"

"Positive."

Ten minutes later we are packed up and making our way back up the one-hundred-yard passage to the cave's exit. My father, Tracy and Lily are leading the way followed by Winston, Warwick, Naomi and Nasya, with Poppy and I in the back. Happy to not be under Alia's control, as there is still no sign of her, yet afraid to act out on his own free will, Kirill shuffles alongside the two of us.

Poppy assures me along the way that everything will be fine with her sister. She suspects Alia is most likely right behind us, yet far enough that we cannot see her.

And although Poppy is probably right I have a bad feeling churning in the pit of my stomach. A feeling that is intensified twofold when everyone suddenly stops short. Because after walking the ninety-one meters to get out of this bunker the only thing awaiting at its end is a solid rock wall.

Chapter Eight
Fools Rush In

"What the what?" Tracy questions.

"This doesn't make sense," I wonder aloud.

"Someone's blocked the exit!" Poppy states.

"Tell us something we don't know!" Tracy sarcastically remarks.

"Shut it!" Poppy retaliates.

"Who would have done such a thing?" Naomi cries.

Kirill snickers before adding, "Who do you think?" When no one answers Kirill continues with, "Come on people - he stayed behind for a reason. To do us all in!"

"Blaze would never do such a thing!" Lily declares.

"How do you know?" Kirill pokes.

"Because not everyone is like you!" Lily barks back.

"Relax. No one here, with the exception of this oaf, thinks Blaze did this," Tracy assures, batting his long lashes at Lily. He's beyond pathetic when he tries to smoodge the ladies. And when it's my own sister it is downright sickening.

But no matter how I feel about it, his swooning is enough to make Lily relax and take a deep breath. She exhales rather loudly before proclaiming, "I need to get out of here," in a much calmer tone.

"Not to worry Lily, Winston and I will make passage," Warwick states. "But you all must back away. Moving these stones could be extremely dangerous."

We all take a back seat to watch Winston and Warwick work their magic. Hands at the ready, both men close their eyes in concentration. The cave begins to creak and moan, with the most eerie noises imaginable reverberating around the cavern. It reminds me of the sound of metal on metal and heavy machinery that I heard while in Baltimore. Then in a flash the clamor ceases. Winston and Warwick have their eyes open, mouths agape.

"What kind of voodoo is this?" Winston asks, leaving me to question, "Why, what's going on?"

"We cannot move them – the boulders – the walls – nothing. It will not budge!" Warwick answers.

"It is as if we were under the sea," Winston adds.

"What does that mean?" I ask.

"Oh my god, this is what Blaze warned us about!" Lily adds. "I should have listened to him. I should have gone with him. This spooky-ass place – it friggin' freaks me out!"

"It's not ideal for me either, but we mustn't lose our heads. There has to be another explanation."

"Like what?" Poppy asks.

"Like we must have gotten turned around or something. That's why Alia didn't follow. Maybe she knew all along we were going the wrong way. I say we backtrack and head out the other passage to find her and the exit."

"Don't have to tell me twice!" Tracy utters. Bouncing on his heels he grabs Lily by her arm, throws it over his shoulder then slides his own arm in and around her waist in one fell swoop. "Don't worry babe, I got your back!" he proclaims, smiling at her.

"That's what I'm worried about!" Lily replies.

"Wha? Oh come on!" Tracy flirtatiously stammers.

"Don't give me that, I'm on to you."

"On to what?"

"You'll take just about any opportunity to make a move, won't you?"

"Hmmmm ... suppose so."

"Ambush in a bar, near death experience, entrapment, what's next?

"We'll see. I figure moments of heightened emotional distress give me the upper hand. Wouldn't you agree?" he teases.

"You're pathetic!" Lily roars, pushing him away.

She sees it too!

My heart begins to accelerate after passing the chamber where we camped for the night. This is the only other passage and within minutes it begins to narrow around us. Underfoot I feel a gradual decline. The air is damp and earthy, much like that of our underground bunker at home and I know in an instant that Blaze was right. What he felt before entering this tomb, I now feel surging through every inch of my being.

Our outlet has been sealed shut and I don't know how much longer I can convince everyone that we are currently hiking the original channel to freedom. Surely, they must have noticed that we've been walking for far too long, felt the slump beneath our feet, smelled the mustier air or had a premonition.

With every step I take it becomes all too clear, hidden within the silence that surrounds our normally boisterous clan. They too know.

There is nothing to say. Nothing more to do than continue our trek and see where it takes us.

My mind races with regret, worry, tension.... This mission is a never-ending cycle of continual stress. A mission that weighs me down - ages me. Not in years but in body and soul. My joints ache and I am perpetually tired. Irritable, crotchety - I feel old, broken and worn.

On top of it all I'm starting to feel sorry for myself, which is not a good thing because it makes me want to cry. Yes, cry! I wonder where the old me has gone to – and if I will ever find him again. The full-on impact of thoughts drumming through my skull has given me a thunderous headache. And when I stop to pinch the bridge of my nose, Poppy slides her hand into mine.

"It'll be okay," she consoles.

I merely squeeze her soft fist in reply. Lord knows I want nothing more than for her words to be true.

An hour passes without any sign from Alia and still there is no exit in sight. Kirill keeps moaning on about his hunger pains, my father is drained, and Naomi and Nasya look like they could use a good rest as well. I'm just about to blow the whistle on our hunt when the trail leads us into a massive cavern three times the size of the one we camped in.

The ceiling is higher than in the tunnel. Stalactites hang

down, mimicking the icicles that dangle off the roof of our cottage in winter. Stalagmites protrude from the ground, gathering in bunches along the floor. Across from us on the far end of the cave stand two archways. One is as dark as the shaft we just emerged from; the other is bathed in a warm inviting light.

Cheers of glee emanate from all around me, echoing off the stone and dirt walls. Tracy, Lily, Naomi, Nasya, and Kirill all begin to race toward the bright illumination, sprinting past me, yet their bodies are in slow motion.

My heart accelerates. Intuition kicks in and it hits me....

Fools rush in.

Its meaning is to attempt things wiser people are more cautious of.

We've been barricaded in a cave against our will, forced to go down the only other passage available in order to find another form of egress, which leads us to the two doors (so to speak) standing before us. One with the lights on. One with the lights off. Naturally one would assume the yellow luster to be that of the sun and run to it.

How convenient for us, right?

Wrong!

"STOP!" I yell, just in the nick of time.

Whether it's the urgency in my voice or the overwhelming loudness of my cry, everyone does just so. And in this moment, as everything appears to be suspended in time, all I can take notice of is Lily's hair flying through the air as she turns to look at me. Her long silver tresses glide over the threshold, dance in the light, swirl in the wind. Then boom! Her mane falls limply to her shoulders, chopped off, as if the opening housed an invisible guillotine that just came crashing down.

A lump the size of a goose egg fills my throat and I find I have to swallow hard three times in order to flush it down so I can speak.

"Do NOT move!"

"Why not, Dmitry? Isn't it the way out?" Naomi asks.

Am I the only one that saw that? I ask myself.

"No. I'm not so sure," I reply through gritted teeth. My arm has sprung forward, hand in the stop position. All I want to do is hold them there. Make sure no one does anything stupid. Sweat beads on my forehead as I whisper, "Something is not right here - trust me."

"He's right. You should all listen to him," a voice rings out.

Alia steps into view from the shadow of the dark corridor left of where Lily, Tracy, Naomi, Nasya and Kirill stand. All eyes fall upon her. Arms still folded over her chest, she surveys each one of us, looking us up and down, trying her best to transmit her feelings, convey the dangers without having to speak another word. I can tell she is displeased with the amount she has already surrendered.

Slowly and quietly she turns, disappearing back down the passage. A moment later Poppy crosses the cavern, vanishing behind her. Then Winston, Warwick, Naomi, Nasya, Jaasin and Kirill. When Lily and Tracy move a safe distance from the gleam I let down my guard and follow along.

Tracy's eyes widen when he takes notice of Lily's shorter mane. Hair that once fell to her waist is now a good eight inches shorter, resting bluntly below her shoulders.

"How in the ... what happened to your hair?" he questions.

"Whaddya mean?" Lily responds, running her hands through her tresses. Her eyes widen and she gasps in horror. "Where did it go?" she cries.

"With the light," I answer, as if they will understand. Of course they don't – I can tell by the look on their perplexed faces. But how do I explain what I saw?

"Just leave it at that," I add in a downhearted tone.

"I like it!" Tracy chimes in. "It looks sexy." Raising an eyebrow, he flashes Lily a playful grin.

"You'd say that if I stuck my finger in an electric socket and looked like the Bride of Frankenstein."

"I've always fancied her."

"For crying out loud, you two!" I complain, then spare myself the sour stomach and sprint forward until I reach Poppy and Alia. Falling in beside them I am momentarily thankful for the silence.

"Where are you taking us?" I ask.

When Alia does not respond a pang of guilt overcomes me. Grabbing her by the hand I beg, "Please Alia, don't do this. Talk to me. I need ...."

"My help?" she interjects.

"Yes."

A loud sigh escapes her tiny frame.

"I'm trying." she replies.

Tugging my hand, she pulls me forward, sprinting through the tunnel until we reach an underground grotto with the most beautiful crystal clear pool I've ever seen.

Abruptly Alia pulls me to her. Nose to nose, eye to eye, she speaks soft but fast, carefully articulating every word so that I do not miss a thing.

"We will camp here for the night. Nothing more. You must set an example. Be strong, relaxed, untroubled. Enjoy the beauty that lies before us for there is nothing here to fear. Sleep well and guide us through the light first thing in the morning."

"But?"

"Don't ask – just do! I will help you but in return you must do for me."

"Anything."

"My sister is fragile."

"I understand."

"You will and you will not."

"I....?"

"Will not talk to me anymore, understand? It's just easier that way!" Her voice rises from a whisper to a soft shout. With a tear in her eye she hastily tosses my hand away and skulks off just as the rest of the team appears.

Oohs and ahs fill the area as everyone parades in behind me, their chatter blending in with the words Alia spoke.

"Look at this place."

"It is a stunning sight, no doubt."

Guide us through the light in the morning.

"Amazing!"

"What is Alia doing? Has she been here all day?"

"The water looks so refreshing."

Be strong, relaxed, untroubled.

"I could use a drink."

"I want to jump in!"

"Do you think it's safe?"

There is nothing here to fear.

My feet dart across the floor, carrying me to the water's edge where I jump up, tuck my knees and cannonball into the pool.

Instantly the crisp water washes away all my apprehension. I break the surface feeling remarkably refreshed.

"Whooo hooo!" I cry out, throwing my wet hair back off my face. Lily looks to Tracy, Tracy looks to Lily and they both take off simultaneously, running toward me. In one fell swoop they plunge into the water. As I did, Lily breaks the surface with a squeal of joy.

Poppy, Naomi and Nasya sit at the water's edge, testing the temperature with their feet before carefully lowering themselves in. Winston and Warwick kneel at the edge bathing their arms and faces, dampening the backs of their necks. Kirill attempts a dive that turns horribly wrong resulting in a belly flop, which causes everyone else to crack up hysterically.

When the laughter dies, all eyes fall upon my father. Pacing back and forth he looks extremely apprehensive. And unlike Alia, who clearly does not want to join in the fun, he makes as if he wants to swim.

I wonder to myself if maybe he can't. I'm just about to ask when Lily shouts, "Come on in, Dad, the water's fine!"

Dad.

The word flew off her tongue so easily, so naturally, and by the look on his face it is everything he wanted to hear. Lily looks positively ecstatic. As a matter of fact, everyone does! And really, that is all I could ask for.

Oh, what the hell!

"Yeah, come on Dad!" I yell, goading him on. Then everyone else rallies, catcalling at him to jump in. He shakes his head, twitches nervously, and even shoos us off with a wave of his hand. But when I catch a shimmer in his eye and see the upward turn of the corner of his mouth I know he's putting on a good show.

He's got everyone eating out of the palm of his hands, begging and chanting for him to change his mind. When he walks away as if he's going to leave the grotto the team boos and cries for him to return and that is just what he does. With the cry of a Samurai warrior he runs full speed and leaps into the water to thunderous applause.

Our time in the water was extraordinary. It allowed us to forget all our worries. Brought us back to adolescence. Allowed us to splash, laugh, dive, float and bond. For my father, it washed away years of grime from the cage. For Lily, Tracy and I it washed away the slime from the frozen lake and for Poppy it washed away the residual dried blood from a time, not so long ago, when I thought I had lost her forever. It not only cleansed our skin but our souls. I climbed out of that pool stronger, ready to face whatever life was going to throw at me.

Jaasin lost years off his appearance when he shaved off his unkempt beard and mustache. Naomi and Nasya then cut his long scraggly hair to just below his ears. Poppy helped pick out some of her dad's old clothing from the rucksack Alia threw together, replacing the tattered beige robes and faded black trousers with a crisp pair of chinos and a white t-shirt. That was the moment my father truly returned. He was his old self, the man I saw in pictures and dreamt about after he had vanished.

Winston and Warwick made a fire for all of us to sit around while we dried off and munched on raw nuts. Alia, though silent, joined in and for once, with the exception of Kirill, it felt like we were a true family.

We did nothing except enjoy the relaxing ambiance surrounding us for quite some time. A lot of unspoken words traveled through meaningful eye contact.

"I have a picture of you," Lily announces, breaking the silence, while gazing through the fire at our father.

"You do?" Jaasin responds.

"Yeah, only one. Orvah took it. She said it was early February or something like that. It was nineteen ninety-two. You were in the snow - a wool cap on your head, scarf up over your mouth."

Lily swirls her finger up around her chin.

"But I could tell from your eyes that you were smiling," she adds. With a faint smile she meekly looks down toward the ground.

"Orvah?" Jaasin whispers.

"Yes, she's my mother."

Jaasin chuckles slightly. "Yes, I know. Your mother - do you always call her that?"

"Orvah?"

"Yes."

"Only when I'm mad at her."

A common thread, I think to myself. *Calling our parents by their first names – because of anger.*

"How often are you mad at her?"

"Lately?"

Jaasin nods.

"It's been four full years, and running."

"That's a long time."

Try nineteen.

"I have my reasons."

"I'm sure you do. And when you are ready will you share them with me?"

Lily nods sheepishly. Slowly she raises her head, looks to our father and asks.

"Why were you in that cage?"

"It's a long story," Jaasin replies.

"And when you're ready – you'll share it with me?"

Jaasin sighs.

"Sadly, I will never be ready to share the reason why."

His statement causes Lily's shoulders to slump. Again, she lowers her gaze to the dirt floor.

"I will never be ready – but I will tell you all the same. Lily my dear, I was locked in that cage..."

He swallows hard.

My sister's eyes rise to meet his.

"I was locked in that cage - for killing the Queen."

Chapter Nine
Jaasin

"What?" Lily questions. Her voice is full of shock and disbelief.

"For killing the Queen."

"Eugenia," Lily whispers. It is not a question or even a statement. Eugenia's name swirled off Lily's tongue like a ghost in the wind - a recollection.

"Yes, Eugenia," Jaasin confirms.

"The most beloved of all beings in Realm because she was the only wife to bear a child. But not without a scandal. She gave birth while the King was married to another."

Lily pauses to think of the name.

"Varina. Even so, the people loved her for the great gift she had bestowed upon the kingdom. Five queens - no heir. Theothantanos wed her the day after Varina's execution and everyone throughout the land rejoiced over the union."

Again, Lily pauses. Her chest heaves with every breath.

"Several years later, Eugenia was murdered in cold blood - in front of the Sovereign himself and the members of the royal court."

Lily finishes murmuring the story she once heard from Blaze. Her eyes flash with fury as the comprehension sets in. Getting to her feet she raises her voice. "You? It was you! – MY father? – a murderer?"

Kirill's brassy voice chortles in the background. Hesitantly Jaasin responds.

"No!"

"You just said you did!"

"No, I – "

"No? Am I missing something here? Which is it? You killed her or you didn't? – Murderer or not? Surely it can't be both!"

Lily swallows hard. Intently she stares into our father's

face as if all the answers lie within the weathered cracks of his skin, sizing him up, trying to read him. Did he? Didn't he?

Jaasin's chin quivers as he searches for something to say but Lily continues before he gets a chance to clarify.

"Never mind, what does it matter anyway? What's done is done."

Lily turns to me, "And you - you knew all along! Pulled me into this Realm against my will to help save a convicted felon! What's the matter with you?"

Raising her voice she rages on, "WHAT'S THE MATTER WITH ALL OF YOU? YOU'RE MORE SCREWED UP THAN MY FAMILY BACK ON EARTH!"

"No, Lily, this is just a whole misunderstanding," Naomi assures.

"Slaying your Monarch is a misunderstanding? See what I'm talking about. You've all got a screw loose or something. Mad as a hatter, I tell you! Believe me, when it comes to being unhinged I know a thing or two about it."

"I AM NOT CRAZY!" Nasya shouts. "Jaasin saved my life! He would NEVER take another."

Having nothing more to say, Lily purses her lips. I haven't known her long but being that we are so similar, I know her well enough. Pissed off and curious. Right now the chip on her shoulder isn't allowing her to inquire about Jaasin and his past. Our father is a complete stranger to her, one she has probably wondered about her whole life, as I did. Naturally she wants to know more about him. Especially how he saved my Aunt Nasya. So, I'll do her this one and start the story without her verbal query.

"Our father was only six years old when Naomi and Nasya were born...."

"Dmitry, my son. It is very kind that you want to vindicate me by telling Lily this story, but I'm afraid this old tale won't prove a thing."

"It is the truth and she should know," Nasya declares.

"And when it is all said and done, she will still have her reservations."

"This you cannot predict," Naomi adds.

"I can, Naomi, because I too have them! Every day for nineteen years I have contemplated the prospect that it was I who indeed killed her!"

Outraged Nasya yells, "It is not possible!" Turning to Lily she pleads, "He is a HEALER. You saw it for yourself. He healed you and Dmitry. He healed me when he was six. SIX YEARS OLD! He is a good boy. I know!"

"But I don't!" Lily responds. "I don't know anything about him or any of you." Turning to Jaasin she continues. "So why don't you just tell me."

Jaasin sighs.

"Alright then."

Slowly our father sits down. When he's good and comfortable he begins with, "You see Lily, my mother had the ability to take life. It was an evil power that plagued her own. She was a beautiful woman with a big heart. The kind of woman that would do anything for anyone and wouldn't hurt a fly, on purpose that is!

"So, imagine having this ticking time bomb inside yourself. A defense mechanism that you just can't shut off! And every time you carried a child to term, contractions would start and that bomb, well it would detonate."

Jaasin stops to wipe a tear from his eye.

"Yet you survived," Lily adds.

"Because he's a healer," Naomi insists.

"Because I'm a healer. It took nine times for her to birth a child strong enough to fight her and survive. She swore after my birth she would never do it again. But sometimes, well - miracles happen."

He pauses briefly to look at Naomi and Nasya, slowly turning his gaze from his sisters to Lily. Then he smiles. I know in an instant that he's not just referring to my aunts. A wave of pins and needles trickle up my spine, followed by guilt. Guilt for having such hatred for the sibling I learned about the day I first reached my father's cage and spilled my blood unsuccess-

REALM: RULER OF THE PEOPLE, GOD OF DEATH

fully. I had such a loathing that he created another, loved another and abandoned me. Now with his words I understand. He too swore he would never do it again. But sometimes the thing you feel highly improbable happens, as it did with Naomi, Nasya and Lily.

"We lived in this little shack in the woods where my father liked to hide out. He was an introverted, peculiar man. Always whispering to himself. Other than farming a small plot in the woods for the benefit of our own nourishment, he never did an honest day of work to provide for his family. My mother, on the other hand, would sew, wash and press laundry for the wealthier town folk.

"It was a long walk into the village, but my mother and I would do it every fortnight to get more linens and stock up on supplies. Swollen belly and all, she lugged baskets upon baskets back and forth while he just sat there twiddling his thumbs. I don't know how she did it, but there was always enough money for us to buy fresh bread and cheeses. She took home some of the finest things. Like this eau de toilette she used to wear. "

Jaasin closes his eyes and inhales.

"Sometimes I can still smell her, even after all these years. Anyway, it was late afternoon and we were on our way home with the day's collection when she fell to the ground.

"Overcome with pain, she lay there screaming and yelling. Writhing in agony, she pleaded for me to help her. I wasn't sure what to do! I was just a kid.

"Then fluid and blood ran from her and I knew it was the baby. I remember shaking so hard because I was unbelievably frightened. Frightened for her, frightened for the baby.

'Jaasin my boy, don't be scared. You must help me. Help your baby brother or sister,' she pleaded.

'What do you want me to do?' I asked her through a face full of tears.

"Her body was in turmoil. I could see it in her eyes every time a wave of labor pains hit. She was involuntarily killing the fetus in order to save her own life, yet she wasn't in mortal distress. My mother tried hard to fight the instinct but eventually knew it was a losing battle. It's hard to push something out when your body is fighting to keep it in, steal it and devour it."

'Take the baby out Jaasin. Take it from me before it is too late!'

"I'd never seen or done such a thing, only heard the women talk about it once or twice around town. I was freaking out! We were on the path at the edge of the forest. Less than ten minutes' time and we would be home and my father could tend to her.

"All I could think about was home. I don't know why I did it but I started to run for the woods, screaming and yelling for my father. If he was out in the garden there was a good chance he would have heard. Seams so ludicrous now.

"My mother's bloodcurdling yelp spun me on my toes and back to her side. 'It's okay, baby. You can do it. Just use the linens,' she instructed. So, I grabbed them, gently sliding a small stack under her hips, then laid another on the dirt floor. The baby's head was already there waiting for me. All I had to do was pull it downward then ease the shoulders out one at a time. The body slipped right out after that onto the sheet and a new cry rang through the air.

"My mother beamed and giggled this giddy little laugh. Through all my sweat, tears and snot I joined in, rejoicing for the new baby girl lying before me. Then it started all over again. My mother began to scream and yell.

'Momma!' I cried. 'Momma!'

'It's happening.' she bellowed.

'What Momma? What's happening to you?'

"But she didn't answer that time, just shrieked in agony. Her breathing became a pant and she started to thrash about. That's when I caught sight of the other head. Another baby was coming. I grabbed hold, as I did before, but this one wouldn't pull free.

'It won't come out!' I remember screaming. My mother's voice was calm and soothing. Something about it sent a wave of chills up my spine. All her torment and suffering and yet she had enough strength to compose herself in order to guide me.

'The baby is stuck Jaasin. It will die if you don't tear it free.'

'But I will hurt you, Momma.'

'Not as much as if the baby dies my son. Now do it.'

"She laid there silent and still, holding her breath, biting her lip. Tears spilled from her eyes like a small river cascading down her cheeks, pooling on the dry soil.

"I felt the bone move as I pressed my hands inside and around the baby's neck. With all the strength I could muster I pulled its body free."

Having said that, Jaasin breaks down crying. Naomi and Nasya each place a hand upon his shoulder for comfort. Lily's eyes are swimming. She is waiting with bated breath for him to continue, which he chooses to do even though he's still weeping.

"But there was no body. Just this shriveled mess of blood and bone. I could see her miniscule heart pounding inside her tiny rib cage. It was growing fainter and fainter as the seconds passed. She did not whimper or cry as the first child had done and when I heard my mother bellow in agony I thought for sure it was because of what was left of the baby in my arms. But I was wrong."

Again, our father pauses to catch his breath and wipe the tears from his eyes.

"It was triplets. My mother carried three babies within her. The first girl was healthy and strong. The second was nothing more than a head upon her shoulders and the third – well the third never had a fighting chance. Like the body of the second baby, it was nothing more than a pile of bloody bones.

"And that is when my mother's culpability reared its ugly head. It was then, in the awareness that her power had yet again caused her to take the innocent lives of the ones she loved most.

"She laid there bleeding and crying, murmuring about her past. How she accidentally killed her best friend as a child, her

71

first love and an occasional animal here and there. Because of it she condemned herself to a life of solitude in the woods with my father. That way she wouldn't hurt anyone else, but it was of no use.

"Her tenth child was dead, another baby lie next to her dying and she looked at me, broken in every way. Her eyes filled with sorrow, loss and guilt. Then she whispered for me to forgive her."

JAASIN

Chapter Ten
Workhouse Squalor

"Then what happened?" Lily asks.

My daughter. What a delicate flower. How I would love to spare her the details of the past. For the story of my life is not one I wish to relive or retell. But she is correct; we do not know each other. This piece of history is essential in order for her to understand who I am and how this all came to be. Swallowing hard, I continue.

"My mother had the ability to take life."

The words were a lot harder to get out then I thought they would be. So, I sit in silence staring longingly into the pool of water trying to collect myself. I know the others are waiting for me to come around but a story like this takes time. Minutes later I try again, my voice trembling with each word.

"The baby in my hands was turning blue. I thought my mother was apologizing for it being moribund. I knew she felt bad about the loss of this life as she did the others, so I started to plead for her to not be upset. I tried to convince her that it would be okay, that I could fix it.

"I wasn't thinking, or I was, but not about the consequences. The baby's body was dead and no matter how hard I tried to heal her she was so far gone there was no coming back. I placed her down next to the healthy girl, held them together and prayed for the baby to heal.

"It was crazy magic but I wanted my mother to know they would be okay. The two babies started to fuse together and then the healthy girl began to turn blue as well. My mother screamed and I let go of them in an instant.

"From the moment I ran back to my mother's side everything simultaneously spiraled out of control. Blood was trickling out of her mouth and I finally understood what she was doing. Why she asked for my forgiveness.

"I started to panic, pleading and crying for her not to do it. For the second time that afternoon I found myself screaming for help. Placing my hands upon her chest, I fought her. I wasn't going to let her go. But she was much more powerful and started to pull me down with her.

"I was growing faint. I felt tired and it was hard for me to concentrate but somehow through all the fog, I could see my father standing over us. He looked down at my mother's lifeless body, grabbed a basket of linens and took off running back into the woods shouting something I couldn't quite make out. The last thing I saw before the darkness took over was an older man and woman running toward us.

"When I came to, the King himself was standing over me. His eyes were an intense golden yellow and they studied me with a combination of displeasure and pity.

'The boy did it!'

"That is what my father yelled as he ran from us and, in turn, that is what the old man and woman told the King. I sat there alone, cold and frightened as they rolled my mother's body up in sheets then loaded her into a stagecoach. Before closing the doors they placed a single small bundle of cloth on top of her chest – my own was about to burst."

I pause to look up at Lily.

"That was the last time I saw her. I don't even know where she was laid to rest. If they even buried her, that is. Theo-thantanos took me by the hand and pulled me up onto his horse without saying one word. I was too scared to talk. I knew with Royalty you never spoke unless spoken to. Worried about the ramifications, I kept my mouth shut.

"I wanted to tell the King what truly happened more than anything. I wanted to scream from the rooftops how my mother took her own life because of her foul ability. How my bloodstained hands were from delivering her babies and trying to save her life. I wanted him to know that my own father was the one who was framing me for her death. How he ran away from us, leaving her there to rot. Left not knowing if his only son would live or die.

"In that moment of explicit sorrow, blinding rage and despair it occurred to me that whatever punishment was in store for a six-year-old murderer was most likely far better than going back to him. So, I never said a thing. I just let my tears wash it all away. The blood, the sorrow, everything but the memory of her."

"Were you imprisoned then?" Lily asks.

"I was – and I wasn't."

"I don't understand."

"The King placed me in a home."

"Like an orphanage?" she questions.

I can't help but snicker. "No, my darling. Back then not many folk would take in a wayward child. An emotionally disturbed and behaviorally delinquent boy wasn't going to luck out with something so glamorous. And especially considering what I'd been accused of.... no, I was sent to a workhouse."

"What's a workhouse?"

"It's a place where people who can't support themselves go to live. In exchange for food and shelter they make you work for them."

"Sounds like a pretty good deal."

"No darling, you are sorely mistaken. The poor unfortunate soul that voluntarily turned up or was sent there would disagree.

"After putting me on his horse, Theothantanos separated from his guards. He told them to ride on without him whilst he dealt with the boy. I was trembling yet curious as we rode on through the dusk. Finally, he stopped at the entrance of a large stone building. Standing there behind a black iron gate stood a brick-red building over three stories tall. Its windows glistened in the twilight.

"I thought it to be the most beautiful palace in all the world. Not that I'd seen anything bigger than the average dwelling before. It was a haven so spectacular, trumping our little shack in the woods. I knew for sure it was the King's castle. How silly of me, but I was, after all, only a child.

"That first night they stripped me of all my clothing and hosed me down in the most inhumane way. I never felt so embarrassed and humbled. Didn't even know what the emotions were at the time.

"I was given a uniform two sizes too big to wear and the only item returned to me was my shoes, which I had to keep until the soles wore through and my toes poked out the front. I was placed in the laundry room. It wasn't bad at first since it reminded me of home. But life at the workhouse was not meant to be comfortable. It was extremely harsh in order to make sure that only the most impoverished person would walk through those doors.

"It was a wretched place full of elderly men and women who could barely walk let alone work. Children as young as three were sent off into the mines to dig for coal; some never did return. I liked to think they escaped, yet over the years I came to realize that most likely wasn't the case.

"We were all beaten and starved. Some children were even sold as slaves, which we were told benefited the rest of us. The money provided to the house gave us food and nourishment. They said we should reflect upon the sale of a child as an advantageous circumstance. Gruel was the most appetizing thing on the menu, and that is saying something. Meat tainted with maggots, bread covered in mold. Heinous doesn't even describe it.

"Disease spread like wildfire. Typhus, tuberculosis, the plague, you name it. By nineteen-eighty everyone I had known had come to pass. And somewhere within those twelve years the workhouse morphed into an infirmary. If you ask me it was more like a morgue.

"On my eighteenth birthday, I was thrown out on the street with nothing more than the clothes on my back."

The recollection causes me to sigh.

"My sweet Lily – Do you understand the picture I have painted for you? Sugar-coated ... yes, but I think you get the point - don't you?"

"Yes and no."

"I gave you the same answer just moments ago. An answer you found unacceptable."

The color in Lily's cheeks begin to rise.

"I...."

"You were right to say the things you said," I interrupt, "you wanted to know if I was a murderer or not, because surely it couldn't be both yes and no. Do you see now how sometimes things are more complex?"

"I'm starting to."

"Good."

I watch as Lily bites her lip while thinking about what she just heard. Trying to picture me growing up in such conditions. Not even knowing there is so much more to learn about my life. If only I could stop the story now.

"Go on," Dmitry coaxes.

Lily's eyes widen in anticipation. I nod, then chuckle.

"It's a funny thing how you can grow so dependent on the thing you despise the most. I fantasized day in and day out about getting out of that place. What it would be like to be free. And once I was, I didn't know what to do with myself! It's completely absurd, but true. I had no home, no money, no food and worst of all, no family.

"I started to think about my father. Turned the events of that day over and over in my mind, wondering how he could leave his newborn babies and wife to die, and frame his son for the murders. I wanted to know what he had done with himself all those years.

"I went from being scared and alone to angry and obsessed. My new mission in life was to track him down, so I started walking. It took me the better part of two days to make my way back to the infamous spot at the edge of the forest. I dropped to my knees and wept. It was the first time I allowed myself to cry since that day all those years ago.

"When I felt strong enough I moved on, wondering with each step how I was going to confront him once I found him. But all the scenarios I played out in my head didn't prepare me for the reality of the situation. The shack, like me, had been abandoned.

"My mother's clothes still hung in the cupboard. Dirty dishes were in the sink. It was a dusty old museum housing the relics of my childhood. Waiting there for me - to remind me - to haunt me. Like a fool, I stayed. Thought it would make me happy to be around her possessions. But in the end material things are not what life is all about and I found myself growing mad in more ways than one.

"For the sheer insanity of trying to recreate a past that no longer existed for me and for the anger that consumed every inch of my being. I tore myself away with the promise that I was going to make my father pay for every wrong he committed.

"It took some time but I was able to piece together enough information to know he had left the island, and moved onto a greater expanse of land to the southeast. I scrounged and begged my way across the sea. Stole, borrowed and bartered anything I could get my hands on for information on his where-abouts, finally pinpointing his location to a large forest. Some-where within he was squirreled away and I was going to find him.

"I left no stone unturned. A week into my search I was still empty-handed. The second week I felt no closer to him than the day I was thrown out of the poorhouse and decided to pursue the endeavor. But the third week – the third week I re-ceived a sign from above."

"You found him?"

"No, she found me."

"Who is she?" Lily questions.

I turn to Dmitry. Lily's eyes follow.

"Eirlys. The love of my life."

The sound of her name brings a smile to my face. Dmitry

grins slightly before lowering his gaze to the ground.

"Oh," Lily murmurs. Thankfully it was an inquisitive groan rather than a depressed grumble.

"I was standing in a small clearing, tired and hungry, when she emerged from the trees, dancing on the air. Her long brown hair glistened in the sun and when she spoke her voice was like heaven.

'There is so much life in this forest. Turn over every rock and it will still not present itself to you, as I have done,' she said to me.

"I didn't know how to respond to that, wasn't even sure what she was talking about. My mind was racing, wondering what kind of creature she could be, for I knew she was not of our world. One look into her sharp emerald eyes and every ounce of anger diminished. Surely, she must be an angel, I thought.

'I don't understand.' I finally replied to her.

'Of course you don't.' She answered, smiling so that I could see her pointed teeth. 'Here, take this.' And she handed me a small parcel.

'What is it?' I asked her.

'It is food. You need to eat.'

'I'm fine.'

'No you're not. You have not nourished your body in days.'

'How do you know that?'

'I have been watching you now for weeks.'

'Weeks?'

'Yes, now eat.'

"She disappeared as fast and as quietly as she arrived yet I knew she was out there somewhere, still watching me. I ate every last bite, built myself a small shelter and slept for the night. In the morning, I awoke with her standing over me. That day she taught me how to forage for food and asked me why I was in her forest.

'Your forest?' I questioned.

'Yes, my forest!'

'I didn't know you were the King.' I proclaimed.

'Don't be silly, I am the princess!'

"For a minute there she had me and I just had to ask...

'The princess who vanished in nineteen fifty-four?'

'Wouldn't you like to know?'

"Yes, the girl before me was very young, but the King's ability was to age slowly or possibly not at all. I'm not exactly sure what his specific power is but theoretically his daughter could have inherited his trait or a similar one. She very well could have been his kin, so I threw out my chest and said in the manliest voice I could muster, 'I'll just have to bring you back to the King so he can tell me himself!'

'You'll have to catch me first!' she teased, coaxing me into a game of chase. Running around after her was the first time in my life that I actually felt like a child. Yet I was a grown man.

"Playfully she threw herself to the ground, collapsing in a heap of what I liked to call 'fake exhaustion' seeing as she was fit as a fiddle. Tumbling down alongside her, I fell in love.

'You're the prettiest princess I've ever seen!' I exclaimed and kissed her quick on the lips.

"Pulling away from me, she folded her knees up under her body, laid her chin upon them and blushingly tucked her hair behind her ear - and that's when I saw it.

'You're an Elf!' I blurted out. I couldn't believe it. All over Realm you hear about them, but they were never to be seen.

'Shhhh!' She hissed back, 'You mustn't know, my father will be so displeased.'

'Why, am I not a presentable enough suitor for your highness?' I teased.

'Suitor, ha!' she laughed.

'Sure, laugh it off, but you're the one chasing me around.'

'Chasing you around? I just want to know what it is you're looking for.'

'In your forest?'

'Right, my forest!'

"I told her everything. Eirlys in turn confided in me. She

told me her father is the ruler of their tribe, so in essence he was a King of their own making. She was not the lost princess, but a princess indeed. The forest I had been roaming was their home for over ten generations."

"So yes, it was HER forest. Right, my son?"

"Yes," Dmitry replies before adding, "She knew more about it than anything in the world, along with the whereabouts of your father."

"And that is how I found him, Lily. Eirlys led me across the river to a small shack just like the one we used to occupy. Sure enough he was out tending to a small garden, just as he did back in the day. Nothing much had changed about him except for his graying hair. Eirlys and I stood there watching for almost an hour until I gathered enough courage to say something. I was just about to approach him when I caught a glimpse of a woman with long dark hair coming out of the cabin.

"I was so angry I didn't know what to do, so I ran back through the woods and into the river to blow off some steam. I couldn't handle the fact that he moved on. I wasn't ready for the prospect and I needed to leave. Eirlys convinced me to stay. She told me that the elves felt that when you were lucky enough to stumble upon love, you should walk with it. If my father found it, I should be accepting. Grabbing me by the arm, she led me to the far edge of the riverbank where we sat in the shade of a large tree until I calmed down.

"It was then that the woman with the dark hair arrived on the other side of the brook. Draped in a brown cloak to ward off the evening chill she carefully bent her petite frame down to gather water into a bucket. In doing so the cloak slipped from her head and I could finally see her face. A face I would recognize anywhere - my mother's!"

Chapter Eleven
The Lord Giveth and He Taketh Away

"I couldn't believe it! There she was looking down at the cool crisp water. I had been mistaken. It wasn't another woman after all, or my mother. It was a child. The most beautiful child I have ever seen, one - with two heads upon her shoulders.

"Instinctively I ran into the water, laughing and crying. I was so happy that two of my sisters were alive that I didn't even think about startling them, which is exactly what I did. They dropped the bucket and took off running."

I pause to look at my sisters most lovingly. Oh, how I admire them so! Naomi decides to use this moment to her advantage by continuing the story from her angle.

"We were so surprised. Besides our father, we had never seen anyone else in the woods before and then all of a sudden there was this handsome boy, well, man, running, yelling and screaming through the middle of the water. We raced back to the cabin and hid inside. Our father always told us that if someone saw our deformity we would be banished to the Melting Pot. I didn't know why he had charged at us and a part of me was scared that he was going to turn us in," she states.

Placing a hand on Lily's leg, she turns her head toward Nasya, who takes over their tale.

"But that is not what frightened us the most. We felt something. Something we'd never felt before. If we told our father that someone had seen us, he would have moved us to another location or would never have allowed us to leave the cabin again. There was something about that man in the forest, and for some reason I knew Naomi and I could trust him. At some point in time we needed to find him again.

"That night after supper there was no water to wash and our father reprimanded Naomi and me for not getting it earlier that day. We had no choice but to go back and get the bucket. When we arrived at the river, we saw that Jaasin and Eirlys were still there waiting for us."

"I didn't tell the girls who I was at first. I was apprehensive about what our father had told them about me. I didn't want to scare them off again," I quickly add.

"The second I saw him standing there I knew. Not that he was our brother, but that he was a healer. I remember feeling this surge of excitement flow through me. Our father told us having an abnormality was bad; having no power was worse but combining the two was deplorable. And now I was feeling a power for the first time."

Naomi smiles with the remembrance before continuing, "Our father always told us that he had the power to keep us safe within the forest and I knew right then and there it was a lie. I identified Jaasin's ability, I knew Eirlys was an Elf; with my father, I felt nothing. I thought I had no ability, when in fact it was he who didn't have one for me to feel!"

Nasya excitedly interjects, "Their aura was good and when we went home that night I could sense our father was not the man he led us to believe. I always had my doubts, but meeting my brother that day validated the sensation I had all along. Every day after that we started sneaking out to see Jaasin and Eirlys."

The reminiscence stirs me from within, awakening a tiny part of me that has been dormant for so long. It enlivens me, bringing a serene smile to my old face.

"There was a lot of running about in those woods back then. Eirlys and I - we fell in love, but seeing as there are no keeping secrets from the Elves our affair was quickly uncovered. Einar, Eirlys's father, was most definitely NOT pleased with his daughter falling in love with a commoner. Thankfully her brother Esben disagreed. He reminded Einar about their faith. If Eirlys was lucky enough to find love, he should at least give me a fighting chance.

"I never met anyone like her in my life. I had forgotten what it was like to feel happiness. Because of Eirlys I was reunited with a part of my family I thought to be forever gone. I was willing to do whatever it took to make her my wife.

I never did return to see my father. In the end, I chose love over hate and for a short while I was better for it. Over time I told Nasya and Naomi about their mother and the true story about her death. I apologized profusely for being the cause of their disfigurement."

"If it wasn't for you I wouldn't even be here," Nasya interrupts, rekindling a long debate between the three of us. It is a subject I should have buried a long time ago but I just can't shake the notion that somewhere deep down they are resentful for the deprivation I have caused them.

"You say that," I mumble.

"We say it, we mean it – we love you Jaasin."

Naomi grabs me under the chin, forcing me to look into her face, and continues, "Look! Look what you have given us." Nasya then points to Dmitry, Lily and then one by one down the line of the rest of the team with the exception of Kirill. "We are all here – because of you!"

I am honored they have all banded together on my behalf and so disheartened that it is again I who will put their lives in jeopardy. A flush of sadness strikes, suppressing my recollected moment of happiness.

"The lord giveth and he taketh away," I reply, water brimming in the corners of my already bloodshot eyes.

"Stop that!" Nasya pleads.

"No, it's true. I gave you life and in doing so took it away!"

"That's enough!" Naomi cries.

"But that is my point! It is NOT enough! You know exactly what I mean. Yes, you are alive and breathing but are you really living? Bottled up in a cabin for forty-three years? Afraid of being deported to the Pot?"

Nasya's forehead crinkles. Enunciating every syllable so that I understand the power and certainty of her words she growls, "I am not afraid - WE are not afraid anymore! We've been there Jaasin. Our road to free you opened that door. We've seen the land and its people – and it is beautiful! We're tired of hiding. Tomorrow we walk out of here with you to face whatever life throws at us!"

"Look at Dmitry," I shout. "HE GIVETH!" I bellow, tears streaming down my cheeks, cascading over my dry parted lips. "And he taketh away!" Placing my hands over my face I curl up into a ball to grieve.

"It is not your fault she is gone," Naomi consoles while rubbing my back.

"I wasn't there to save her. If I never left...."

"How were you to know, how were any of us to know?"

But in a way, we all did. I knew he had it in him - I just never conceived him to be a threat.

"What happened?" I can hear Lily whisper to my right. Sympathetically Naomi replies, "Nasya and I kept our relationship with Jaasin a secret from our father. We were teenagers and the defiance was so thrilling. We felt alive when we were with our brother. It was normal for us to meander through the forest, so slipping away for an hour to see him here and there was easy.

"It started out small. Little picnics while we picked berries, stories by the water while we fished for the day; carefully we incorporated our daily chores into our time together.

"Watching Jaasin and Eirlys fall in love was pure magic. He wasn't Elfish so he couldn't follow the tribe. Lord knows he's not light of foot! So naturally he did the only thing he knew how to do, laundered and pressed linens and clothing for money. Before long we were spending our days helping him build a house for his bride-to-be; the very bungalow in which we all still live."

The thought of seeing it again warms my spirits, if only a little, and I pull my hands away from my face as Nasya continues where Naomi left off.

"Our chores were neglected more and more as time went on. The cottage was built, Jaasin and Eirlys married. Our father scolded us for being rebellious teenagers but neither Naomi nor I cared. It was a great excuse for us to continue on with our little escapade. And over time I suppose we got sloppy covering our tracks. Dmitry was born and we both found it hard to stay away from the people that brought us so much joy.

"It was late December and a light dusting of snow covered the ground. Dmitry was two and a half years old by then and just the cutest little thing you could imagine! Naturally we wanted to spend every waking moment with him. Jaasin had left the night before to travel into the city. He was going to surprise Eirlys with a new dress for the holidays, so Naomi and I dressed before the sun in order to spend a full day with our sister-in-law and nephew.

"But instead of slipping out unnoticed that morning, as we had done so many mornings before, our father was already awake, waiting for us outside the cabin door. He had been suspicious about our behavior and decided to investigate. He knew all about Jaasin and was furious with our deception. He forced Naomi and I back into the shack, bound us to a chair, barricaded the door and lit the shack on fire."

"Oh my!" Lily gasps.

Dmitry bites his lip.

The loathing I feel toward that man even after all these years sends a fury through my veins so powerful it gives me the strength to speak once more.

"He left Naomi and Nasya to die, then went after my family and I. The only thing was, I wasn't home. By the time I got back, Eirlys was gone. There was no way for me to save her. Einar was the one that heard her muffled cry; when he arrived at the cottage she lay there motionless in the snow. My father was fleeing the scene with Dmitry in his arms.

"I don't know what went so wrong that day - why Eirlys didn't take Dmitry and disappear. It's impossible to sneak up on an Elf because they can hear for miles. There is no way she heard my father's footsteps and assumed it to be Naomi and Nasya. She could identify the differences between the girls and me, the way they shuffle slightly after every fourth step opposed to my flat-footed stomp.

"Maybe Eirlys thought I was returning home a little early. I can't tell you for sure but deep down in my gut I know my father didn't intend to surprise her at all. I think he walked there and introduced himself. Befriended her before putting his hands around her precious neck. Either way I am told Einar's revenge was nothing short of barbaric.

"Thankfully Esben, Leif and Kara smelled the smoke on the air and pulled Naomi and Nasya to safety. Their hovel was destroyed, along with the new life I had created for myself.

"Naomi and Nasya settled into the cottage with me and took over caring for Dmitry. It was supposed to be a time of celebration but here we were performing a burial for my dear love. I was so overcome with the loss. I tried – so very hard - to keep it together. For my sisters – and my son. But I was unraveling so fast. I just needed to get away. So, I left."

Having said that I turn to Dmitry and gaze at the grown man before me. "My deepest regret is not being there for you. I am so sorry, my son. I never meant to abandon you as my father did to me. All I wanted that day was some space and time, without all of the perpetual hardships my life had been so full of. I needed to be without the supernatural, I needed a place - to feel whole – to feel human."

Swallowing hard, Dmitry croaks out, "I understand, "which I know he really doesn't. Having been through it myself there are feelings of inadequacy, indignation, rejection and in his case - jealousy.

They are all emotions he has acted out on his journey to free me and in the days since. There is so much more I want to say to him in order to right my wrong. This next part of my past he will not be pleased with but it is essential for him to hear.

Smiling gingerly I continue, "I registered at Customs and crossed over into Earth. For a week I bummed around the streets of Baltimore, sleeping on park benches and eating trash. The change of scenery didn't do a thing, probably because of how I went about it. You live like dirt, you're going to feel like it.

"There was this part of me that needed to heal and I didn't have the power to do so. I started to feel worse, even contemplated taking my own life just to be with Eirlys again. That's the downfall of my ability; the physical part of me would heal itself, making suicide so difficult. Frankly I didn't have the energy.

"Deep down I knew I was crazy; a part of Eirlys was still alive and well in Dmitry. I had to fix what was broken within me so I could go home and see my son again. That night I admitted myself - well tried to admit myself - to a psychiatric ward."

Sighing deeply I whisper, "Orvah."

Her name on the wind makes Lily smile. Dmitry on the other hand purses his lips. I would like to tread lightly for his sake, but what happened between the two of us was so extraordinary, I can't.

"Tranquility and warmth just radiated from her. I felt the glow the second I stumbled through the door and gazed into her ebony eyes. I was spellbound when she took me by the hand and bought me a cup of coffee instead of admitting me as a patient.

"When I spoke to her it was as if she knew everything that I was thinking. As if she had experienced the loss of Eirlys alongside me. I don't know how Orvah did it but she saved me. Pulling me into her light she stopped me from drowning in a sea of darkness. I didn't expect to fall in love again."

I pause for a moment to give Dmitry a minute to react. When his eyes lighten, I know it is all right for me to continue.

"It tore me in two. There was so much more Orvah didn't know about me that I couldn't tell. She was so whimsical and spiritual I thought for sure the gateway to Realm would show itself and I could take her back with me and introduce her to my child, who I missed so much. I was ready to go back to him and at the same time I couldn't leave her.

"Every morning I awoke with anticipation, swearing it would be the day she saw. I could have forced it on her, but what would be the point if she didn't believe? Patiently I waited but it never seemed to happen, and then one night she fell.

"She was hurt, not badly but I still didn't like to see her discomfort, and when I touched her it just – it just happened. Two men materialized into the night and took me back to

Realm, throwing me into a heap onto the stone-cold floor.

"For the second time in my life I found the King standing over me, his expression the same as it had been all those years ago. Except this time he was frowning down upon a man. It was an odd moment looking up at my superior, a man who hadn't aged a day in those twenty-four years since our last encounter. Yet standing right next to him was his wife Eugenia who looked like she was well into her late sixties.

"I was confused as they stood before me. Surely the small bit of magic I did was a misdemeanor. I was so angry that healing Orvah's twisted ankle managed to land me before the Sovereign, leaving her out there in the middle of Patterson Park all alone. She was probably scared to death.

"When Theothantanos opened his mouth to speak I felt a rage of fury surge through my veins. I wanted nothing more than to squeeze the very life from his limbs for all that he had done to me. And at that precise moment the Queen bent down, lowering her hand for me to take, insisting I stand before the King addressed me.

"The second she took my hand into hers the smile upon her face changed abruptly to shock. Breathing hard she stared at me with wild eyes. My own heart accelerated for I didn't know what was happening. Then she looked at the King and grabbed him forcefully by the hand.

"Theothantanos cupped his other hand over hers. I wasn't sure if he was trying to pry the queen's hand from his own or comfort her, because all the while he kept shouting, 'NO! – NO – NO – NO – Don't do it Eugenia, don't do it! – You promised you would never do it!'

"The queen began to shake as if she were being electrocuted. Through gritted teeth she tried to reply but only managed to get out, 'You!' before her body started to wither and shrivel. It was as if the King and Queen were in the midst of some kind of battle with me tangled up in the middle.

"At first I tried to pull my hand free but her grip was still so strong. Then I figured if she was in such duress I should be

JESSICA CANTWELL

saving her, so I tried – tried so very hard to heal her. But I wasn't
strong enough. Her eyes rolled back and her body began to cave
in. When the King let go of her hand she fell forward right on top
of me. The two of us toppled to the ground, her body pinning
me to the floor like a rotted hollow log.

"I was nose to nose with her dehydrated, sunken face, laying there staring into empty eye sockets. Shock turned to panic
and I freaked out. Pushing her off me I threw up all over the floor.
In all my life, all the death I have seen - nothing was as horrifying
as that moment."

Chapter Twelve
Caricorpion

Though it is weightless, silence falls heavily in the cavern, blanketing us with a force so powerful we have no choice but to surrender to the depths of our core where thoughts churn in our guts. And the feeling I get, the feeling I have always felt from that day is the same - doubt.

"So, you see, I very well could have done it."

"You're a healer," Naomi whispers.

"And our mother was not."

"You are not her," Nasya insists.

"Yet we are from the same flesh."

"As are we. Death - Life (she points to me) – Perception (to her and Naomi) – Momentum (to Dmitry)- Dissolve (Lily). We are all so different."

"I was very angry," I murmur.

My words disappear into the hush. I know what they are thinking. Silence tells a person so much. They are pondering the possibilities. Am I their loving brother – father? Everyone has secrets, what could I be hiding from them? Am I capable? Am I a monster?

Monster? I begin to mull it over myself. The word manifests into a series of questions, questions I don't even know how to answer. For example, who am I? What is the definition of me? I have been an animal, caged for so long that I don't even know if a person exists.

What I do know is that I am a disease, tainting everyone I come in contact with. And here standing before me are the four most precious people I have left in my life. Naomi, Nasya, Dmitry and Lily. I had less than a decade to bond with my sisters, two and a half years with Dmitry, which he possibly can't remember, and just the last few hours with Lily.

They don't know me. Hell, I don't even know myself. My heart sinks and I turn my back to them, walking away from this vault, back toward the light.

"I have been that angry too," A small voice echoes. The sincerity stops me in my tracks.

"I've been that angry for a long time. Too long! And the only person I have ever hurt – was myself."

I turn back, gazing into the face of my beautiful daughter.

"Oh Lily." My heart drops once more.

"I don't want to feel that way anymore and I don't want you to feel that way anymore. I don't care if you did it."

"But what if I did?"

"You probably didn't!"

"I will never be certain."

"And I am fine with that. But I am not fine with you walking out that door."

"Oh darling!" And I rush to her, gathering her tiny frame into my old weathered arms. "Thank you!" I chant.

Dmitry stands and I grab him, pulling him in as well. Holding both my children I swear, "I will never leave you two again!"

Dmitry squeezes me tight and Lily sniffles, burying her face into my neck. I breathe the two of them in and whisper, "I promise! – Never again."

That night I slept better than I had in over a decade. I arose feeling rejuvenated and stronger. Forty-nine years of life and I spent the last sixteen of them feeling as if the digits were reversed and I was ninety-four. It is high time my body gives back. I am famished and ready for the next step in this endeavor.

Looks like I'm not the only one. The lot of us is awake with the exception of Kirill. The bags have been packed and Dmitry is pacing the center of the cave with his fingers pressing the bridge of his nose.

"Are you alright, my son?" I ask.

He sighs heftily before answering, "I'm just a little apprehensive that's all. I'm not sure what's going to happen next." He takes two more strides before clapping his hands together and shouting, "Come on everyone, let's move!"

On cue everyone falls in, following Dmitry to the threshold of the grotto.

"Dmitry!" a small yet powerful voice cries out. He turns, eyes wide. Alia is standing there with her arms still folded over her chest.

"Yes?" Dmitry snaps.

Hell-bent on not speaking, she taps her foot impatiently to the ground near the overgrown sleeping swine.

"Leave him for all I care."

Her hiss of disapproval is three times her size. Rolling her eyes, she grunts through gritted teeth, "He knows the location of the other safe haven and whether Theothantanos has a tracker or not. Trust me when I say, YOU NEED HIM, like it or not!"

"Thank you for pointing that out!" Dmitry growls. Marching over to Kirill he kicks the beast twice demanding that he, "Move it or lose it!"

Back out into the holding area we are face to face with the three tunnels, the dark one in which we just emerged, the one in which we traveled yesterday to get here, and the third filled with a lustrous light.

Dmitry stops and holds out his arm motioning with his hand for the rest of us to halt. He turns toward us swallowing hard, "Stay close, stay together - be prepared." He turns on his heel and marches into the light.

The illumination is so bright it brings tears to my eyes. Gold turns to pale yellow and the walls, ceiling and floor begin to dissipate, fading into an effulgent white.

I can see a shadow through my watery eyes. It is round and dark like a floating orb. It takes me back to when I was a child and used to run from outside in the warm sunlight into our dark cabin, purposely causing momentarily blindness. Bubbles of light and shadows danced psychedelically in front of me until my eyes adjusted. Being amazed by the simple magic was such a treat.

Today I am experiencing the same feeling only the

shadow is growing larger, more pronounced. It isn't as round as I initially thought, forming into a silhouette of a large cat with pointed ears. I fear my eyes are playing tricks on me and blink them several times to shake the image away, to no avail. When the hair rises on the back of my neck I know what lies ahead is not a trick or a treat.

It is a Caricorpion, a legendary species I've only heard of in old fables. Their existence has been disputed for centuries largely because they have never been sighted. Folklore has dubbed the Caricorpion as the kiss of death, saying that once you come face to face with one it is the last thing you will ever see.

Over time very few men and women have come forward to chronicle their encounters, describing the animal as a lynx hybrid and penning its tale.

Sure enough sitting before us is a medium-size cat with tall pointed ears that have tufts of black hair at the tips. A beautiful lynx with two large padded paws in front.

But this Caricorpion is no ordinary cat. The torso of this animal turns from a soft coat of medium golden brown fur into a hard-armored shell. It has two large lobster-like pincers, followed by three more legs down each side of its long-segmented tail, ending with a large stinger.

I don't know if it is venomous but I sure as hell don't want to find out. Swallowing the dry lump in my throat I place my hand on Dmitry's back and grab Lily by the hand. The Caricorpion stares intently at Alia with its piercing Peridot eyes. Slowly its head moves from Alia to Dmitry. Its mouth opens slowly revealing a set of razor-sharp teeth.

I watch as the animal shifts its weight, watch its belly tighten, its chest expand. My pulse races in anticipation, expecting the cat to pounce even though it is not in a crouching position. But instead a soft purr rolls off its tongue, followed by smooth seductive words.

"Most unfortunate
To make a bad situation worse

By hiding in a cave with a curse
For every day that you stay
With flesh, you must pay
Right here, right now
And I will tell you how
Today you owe me one of ten
For seeking solace in my den.
Make the sacrifice and the rest may pass
To frolic out in the warm lustrous grass
Nine will walk free to dance and sing
Unless, however, you get caught by the King!
But if you choose to remain
Eventually you'll all be slain."

The beast is right. We have made a bad situation worse by coming here. Blaze sensed it and tried to warn Lily. If only we had listened. Now we are caught between a rock and a hard place. "Today you owe me one of ten." It must be counting Naomi and Nasya as one. "For every day we stay, with flesh we must pay." Meaning, if we wait until tomorrow we owe her two. One alone is too many. There is no other choice but to push forward. But who do we leave behind?

Dmitry turns to the group, not saying a word. His eyes do all the talking as he looks at us one by one in turn. I don't know him well but I do know that he isn't barbaric enough to force the traitor to stay behind, no matter how much he wishes to do so. No matter how we all wish to do so!

He will not spare a single woman or child. To take one brother from another would be inconceivable. Nor would he be able to relinquish his own best friend. The sole purpose of this mission was to save me, which leaves only himself for the taking.

I can see this thought process playing over his strong beautiful face, the face of a child that has not yet grown into a man. A face so full of shock, anger, fright, sorrow, determination and honor.

He opens his mouth to speak and I brace myself not to buckle under the weight of his impending words.

"I'm staying!"

The voice is strong, adamant and most certainly not Dmitry's.

"Tracy -" Dmitry begins to argue.

"It's not up for debate, Dmitry."

"No!" Lily cries. "You can't - I won't let you. Dmitry, don't let him!"

"Lily's right, Tracy. I can't leave without you." Dmitry quavers at the thought of leaving his best mate behind.

Panic brims in Lily's voice as she refuses Tracy's request to sacrifice himself. "If anyone is to be slaughtered by the beast before us, it should be Kirill. Make him stay and pay the price for his sins."

"And in doing that, we would be no better than he." Tracy replies. Suppressing the urge to cry while preventing his body from trembling, he pleads through gritted teeth. "I've made my decision. Don't make this any harder than this has to be. Now go!" Tracy orders, pointing past the Caricorpion to the warm sunlight beyond.

Dmitry closes his mouth, nods to his best friend with eyes full of tears, and turns to face the monster who is now smirking the most salacious smile.

"How brave for you young child
But I am an animal that is wild
This isn't a decision for you to make
It is I who will choose who to take."

My stomach dips, Naomi and Nasya wince and Lily vanishes within my grasp. I feel Dmitry inhale deeply as his shoulder muscles tighten.

"So be it," Dmitry humbly murmurs.

The cat's reflective eyes twinkle as she gazes into Dmitry's. Light begins to radiate from within them, blinding us once again. For a second time my eyes begin to water but I refuse to close them. The Caricorpion's tail twitches, then her shoulders crouch. Her claws begin to snap as she toys with us, gazing from one to another then back to Dmitry. It is a true game of cat and mouse. I clench down upon Lily's hand as hard as I can. One, to let her know I will never let her go and two, to reassure myself that she is still there since I can no longer see her.

In a split second the cat's head snaps toward Alia, her eyes gleam and the soft purr transforms into a wild roar. The silhouette of her frame grows darker as the light begins to brighten, engulfing us in a sea of white. White floors, white walls, white noise. The last thing I see are her eyes on mine, her satisfied grin, her tail swinging forward and her shadow lunge....

Then I ran. Ran as fast as I could into the lambency.

My eyes began to bubble. Black orbs and grey shadows swirl about making me dizzy. My retinas throb, my head and heart pound as a wave of heat surges over my body. I can feel sweat beading across the surface of my dry skin followed by a striking blow to my right knee.

I have fallen. It occurs to me that in doing so I have let go of Lily's hand. I scramble to my feet as quickly as I can, trying with all my might not to panic. Determined to find her, I open my eyes. Though the vision is blurry I can make out a shadow. Instinctively I run to her, grab her by the shoulders and throw her into my arms.

"Jaasin! Thank god you're alright!" Naomi cries.

Pushing her back to arms' length I now see the figure I grabbed was my sisters.

"Naomi! Nasya! Where's Lily?" I yell.

"I haven't seen her," Nasya replies and it hits me. No one can. She disappeared in the cave when she was frightened.

"Lily! Lily!" I scream, frantically grabbing at the air surrounding me, hoping against all hope that I take hold of her.

"Dad!"

Dmitry rushes over with Poppy in his arms. Gently he lowers her to the ground then pulls me into a hug.

"Dad," He whispers.

"My son," I whimper back.

"I went back for you. But once you come out, you can't go back in."

Morosely I nod.

"What's wrong?"

"It's Lily. Somewhere I let go of her hand."

Dmitry looks around.

"No!" I yell in frustration. Gazing around I notice my eyes begin to focus, yet still not as sharply as I would like.

"Damn my eyes!" Dmitry growls.

"I know, mine too." I pant, "But it won't do you any good. Lily became invisible the second the Caricorpion made clear of her plan to hunt. I took her hand … I let go."

"It's okay dad, it's okay."

"We will help you look for her," Winston's voice cuts in. Behind him is Warwick.

I push them aside as trepidation takes over. Naomi, Nasya, Dmitry, Poppy. Now Winston and Warwick. Lily has a one in four chance of survival. Tears stream down my cheeks. Desperately I cry out for her.

"LI-LEEE, LI-LEEE?"

Zig zagging in the hot sun, pushing Dmitry and Poppy aside, I stumble over a large rock once again.

"Damn it!" I curse in frustration, "Lily where are you? LIIIIILLLEEEEEE!"

"I've got her!" a voice calls out.

To my right Tracy stands cradling what appears to be nothing but air in his arms. Softly his hand moves up and down, apparently stroking her hair while he gently coos into her ear, "It's alright, it's alright – I've got you now – You're safe – It's alright."

Pulling myself up once again I rush to her, grab both her and Tracy then pull the two of them into me.

"My darling, I'm so sorry! I didn't mean to let you go."

Her soft sniffle breaks the silence. "It's not that. I thought when you let go…." Her voice begins to crack. "I thought – I

REALM: RULER OF THE PEOPLE, GOD OF DEATH

thought – I thought she took you."

"No honey no, I'm here. I'm fine. Dmitry's fine too. Naomi and Nasya - we're all here."

Slowly Lily begins to reappear.

"Then who?" she asks.

It is a grave question; one I wish we didn't have to answer. But the time has come to find out. Slowly Dmitry gazes from one person to the next, taking attendance of his team. There's Poppy, Naomi, Nasya, Winston, Warwick, Tracy, Lily, me, and of course himself. Only two are absent and only one will join us. Quietly we all turn to see who was the last person to exit the cave.

Chapter Thirteen
Nine

Standing at the mouth of the tunnel is none other than that paunchy snake in the grass, Kirill. Doubled over he heaves his rotund chest, wheezing as he gasps for air then reclines his mass against the rock in order to rest.

"NOOOOOOOO!" Poppy howls into the morning air. Her gulping cry sends a fresh wave of goose bumps up my flesh.

Through all her fire, I saw strength and yet - the little one did not make it through in the end. Poppy's bloodcurdling shrieks stab the morning air. Pushing Dmitry aside, she hurls herself toward the cave running full force until she slams into something the naked eye cannot see. Her body bounces back and falls to the floor causing her to yelp like a wounded animal which is quickly followed by a high pitched, "NOOOOOOOOO!" so full of sorrow it resonates down into my soul.

The exit must be a mirage. Dmitry said it himself. He couldn't go back in to help me. And though there is not much to be thankful for at the moment, I say a little prayer to the lord for it being this way. Going in right now would do us no better.

Since our arrival here at this range we have lost two members. One departed on his own free will, the other stolen from us, and I dare say - much too early. With the exception of Kirill, nine of us remain. How long before the number dwindles to eight … seven … six?

I watch as Poppy struggles to pick her battered body up off the ground. She then throws her weight up against the rock. Cheek to cheek with the cold hard stone she exhaustedly pounds against the optical illusion of an entrance. Relentlessly she laments for her baby sister, crying and crying until her voice grows hoarse while her hands tear and bleed under the strain of her pounding.

Gently Dmitry grabs Poppy's hands, stopping her from causing any further damage. His body pins her in place against the mountain, forming a protective cocoon. At first she fights back, resisting his attempts to calm her then crumbles like a house of cards. Together they weep for Alia against the large tombstone.

My lord, look at what this loss has done.

Tracy has fallen to his knees. His torso is rolled forward into a sort of fetal position. His chin is tucked tightly into his chest and his sobs are silent but I can tell he is crying because of the way his body convulses. Tracy's fists continually grip the earth, pulling great heaps of grass, dirt and sand into his palms before letting it cascade through his fingers.

Naomi and Nasya have taken comfort in Winston and Warwick's arms, burring their faces deep into each dark heaving chest. Lily squeezes my hand as I suppress a small sob. Even Kirill appears thunderstruck and grave with a small tear beading in the corner of his eye. Gently he places a hand upon Poppy's shoulder. It's as odd as seeing snow in July but, nevertheless, it's nice to see he too has a heart.

Poppy flinches at his touch, angrily pulling away, causing Kirill's hand to fall.

"How dare you touch me!" she cries.

Clearing his throat, Kirill growls, "Sad, yes - but you fools are wasting precious time."

"I don't care – just SHUT UP!" Poppy barks.

"You can't tell me what to do! You're not in control of me!"

"I'll kill you – "

"With your bubble, I suppose!"

"Alright Kirill, enough," Dmitry reprimands.

"You can stay here as long as you want crying and blubbering on about that little witch. She's not coming back!"

"IT SHOULD HAVE BEEN YOU!" Poppy yells.

"Tell me how you truly feel, why don't you?" Kirill grumbles.

"YOU BASTARD!" Poppy screams. She pulls her hand free from Dmitry's then smacks Kirill hard across the face.

101

Kirill grunts, holds his palm against the burning sting and retaliates through gritted teeth with nothing more than, "I'll be leaving now."

"You're not going anywhere," Winston growls.

Both he and Warwick have left Naomi and Nasya's side to stand behind Kirill. When the traitor turns to Winton he and Warwick each pull a large machete from the sleeve of their Grand Boubous.

"Not without us," Winston finishes.

Kirill's gloating smile fades to a tight-lipped smirk.

"I refuse to stand out here in the open with you treasonous scum. If you insist upon holding me hostage, we must get to the next safe haven. NOW!"

"Cause this one was so safe! I'm not walking into another one of your deathtraps, thank you!" Tracy spits.

"I did not know," Kirill responds.

"I did not know, I did not know!" Tracy mocks before growling, "What do you know?" His fists wrap tight around another clump of sand and dirt.

"The other blind spot is about fourteen kilometers away."

"And?" Tracy questions as he rises to his feet.

"And what?" Kirill responds.

"What's waiting for us there?"

"Again, I do not know."

"Damn it!" Tracy yells, throwing the contents from his hands and kicking the ground. "I'm sorry – I just can't do it!" he mutters.

"It's a leap of faith, Tracy, but Alia said we needed him. And to a certain extent, we do. Let's honor her wish."

"Need him for what exactly?"

"To tell us whether we are being tracked or not."

"Well, are we?" Tracy questions.

"No," Kirill rumbles.

"Good! There you have it. Honored the wish – now I'm done!"

"But what will we do when Theothantanos finds a tracker,

Tracy?"

"I don't know, Dmitry, what are we going to do? It's sure as hell not going to be sitting around in some cave, getting picked off one by one – one day at a time until we're all gone. Kind of defeats the purpose of this whole mission in the first place. Pull your father out of one cage just to sit and rot in another?"

"What else can we do? He will be killed!"

"Trust Kirill and we will all be killed! - Alia..." Tracy's voice quivers, "case in point!" he whispers.

There is a moment of silence before Tracy continues, "Now, if you'll excuse me - I've had about all I can take for one day. I'm outta here."

Tracy turns and ambles off down the hill with his shoulders slumped forward, his head hung low, looking every bit a man who's carrying a heavy burden along with him.

"Come on Tracy, don't do this!" Dmitry calls after him, "Damn it Tracy!"

"He's right, you know. Your King will continue to hunt us. And we cannot hide forever," Lily states.

"I don't know what else to do," Dmitry responds. "If only I had more time to think."

"I'm sorry Dmitry, I just can't let him go alone."

Lily lets go of my hand and runs to Tracy's side leaving my palm feeling more than empty. I want to follow her but again I am torn between my children. I gaze to Dmitry, looking for an answer, but it is Kirill who breaks the silence. "He refuses to go to safe haven, yet he paves the way."

Dmitry's eyes light up with the notion that Tracy is unknowingly and unwillingly leading us in the direction of the second blind spot, whatever it may be. Perhaps this will be the time he needs, we all need, to think things through.

For three hours we walk through green, lush, mountain down into a golden, grassy plain in almost one-hundred-degree heat. The air is humid and feels thick around my face. I'm finding it hard to breathe and our pace is slowing drastically. Our last bit of water is running low and exhaustion is starting to set in. So much so that when a town full of white stone buildings and large temples appear I quickly dismiss it as another mirage.

Tracy and Lily are the first to reach civilization, quickly joining the crowds of dark-haired, dark-skinned individuals walking barefoot over the earthen ground.

Kirill holds out his hands, motioning for everyone else to stop.

"What is it?" Dmitry questions.

Pulling out a piece of parchment Kirill responds, "This village, it – it must be the blank spot."

Kirill points to the map, "See here? Seven dots - no blondes – yet there they are." He then points to Tracy and Lily who are strolling hand in hand down a dirt path. "I checked the map several times. There were no buildings, no dots beside our own, yet a bustling town full of people stands before us."

"Tracy! Lily!" Dmitry calls, his voice raspy in the excessive heat. Tracy raises his arm, casually waving his hand in the air in a *yeah - yeah* fashion and continues to walk away.

"They entered the village without knowing it was the blind spot. What if it's just like the cave? Can they get out? Will they be able to leave?" Dmitry questions.

"I will not take blame!"

"What do you mean, you won't take blame? Can they get out Kirill?" Dmitry's voice rises.

"They crossed the invisible barrier before I was aware – before I was sure."

"Tracy!" Dmitry hollers. Tracy continues to ignore him.

"Lily!" he cries.

I can tell by the way her body tenses that she hears his plea, understands the urgency in her brother's tone. Softly she tugs on Tracy's hand. He stops and together they turn toward us.

Whether it is from grief, dehydration, exhaustion, a combination of all three, or for dramatic effect, Dmitry collapses. I'm on him before his body hits the ground. Gently lowering his weight down with the help of Winston, Warwick and....

"Tracy?" I whisper in awe. "Where's -" But I don't have to finish the question. Lily is at her brother's side as well, stroking his forehead. A huge wave of relief hits and I find myself hoarsely chuckling an insane little laugh. Dmitry's eyes open and he too snickers wearily.

"If this was a trick to get me to come back!"

"No, no my boy – you and Lily, you entered the safe haven."

"What are you talking about, what safe haven?"

"The second blind spot – it's the village!" I point out. "You were leading us there this whole time! The two of you went in before Kirill realized that the town was the void on his map. Dmitry was concerned that you and Lily...."

"Would be stuck?" Lily finishes.

"Or worse," Dmitry croaks.

Instinctively Tracy pats his body down then looks to Lily.

"I suppose we're alright."

"Thank the lord for that!" I murmur.

"Should we go back?" Lily asks.

"I don't see why not, nothing happened the first time," Tracy adds.

"I don't know...." Dmitry starts.

"Are you alright?" an angelic voice cuts in.

Everyone turns, seeking the source of the divine utterance. There on her knees at Dmitry's feet is a beautiful young girl about the same age as Lily. Concern is spread across her brown face. Her charcoal eyes are soft and kind and her long straight black hair drapes forward framing her face as if it were a smooth silk scarf.

All eyes are upon her and when she speaks again it is heavenly. "I saw you fall, are you okay?" she asks Dmitry.

"Fine – I'm fine," Dmitry stutters then slowly begins to sit up.

"Not too fast," She chides. "You look like you have seen better days."

"Not recently," Dmitry mutters.

"You poor thing. Here, let me help you up." She slides around Winston and up under Dmitry's arm in one quick fluid motion.

Once Dmitry is back on his feet the girl holds out her hand for him to take. "I am Sabeena."

"Dmitry."

"My family and I have a farm about eight kilometers past the other side of town where we grow Kharif crops. You are not from around here, are you?"

"No."

"Looks like you could all use a good meal."

"Yes."

"Come - I own a guest house here in the village – let me feed you."

Gently she tugs on Dmitry's elbow and grabs Poppy's hand in her other, walking them toward the village. Hesitantly Dmitry pulls back.

"It is okay. Wherever you have been, whatever you have been through, you are safe now - nothing to fear. This land here is sacred, the air will protect you, its provisions will heal you – you will see."

I can tell Dmitry likes Sabeena, that he feels he can trust her. Without a doubt, he gives in to her promise, allowing her to shepherd us all into the unknown. Into the town, past the merchants peddling sugar, milk, fish, rice and spices. The air is pungent with the aroma of curry. Men wear turbans and chew on raw sugar cane. Goats and camels walk about.

The women sell jewelry and clothing in the most vibrant shades just like the Ghagra Choli Sabeena is wearing. Her top is bright tangerine orange. It is a soft cotton with white embroidery that clings to her torso and exposes her toned midriff. Her skirt is a long-pleated magenta with gold jewels. She reminds me of Orvah, the way she scooped me up when I was down. Took me out for that cup of coffee.

"What?" Lily questions as we walk along. I gaze at her

questioningly.

"You're smiling," she continues.

"Nothing."

"Come now."

"No – really it's nothing," I insist.

Yet it is everything. Sabeena's mannerism combined with Lily's presence makes me realize how much I miss Orvah. How I long to see her face, smell her scent, run my hands through her wavy hair, even kiss her lips. But I'm kidding myself. Surely, she has moved on. No longer mine for the taking.

Anger begins to bubble in my veins, which is so silly after all this time. And it dawns on me that anger is most likely the feeling she has toward me, for leaving her there alone and cold that night in Patterson Park. For never returning to her and our child.

My thoughts turn over and over, occupying me through the tour of the village until we come to a large grey three-story building. The first floor has three huge mint-green arches with intricately carved art on each pillar. Pocketbooks, umbrellas and other textiles are hanging from the bottoms of the second story jharokhas.

There are checkered tiles out on the sidewalk that extend in through the open arches to an open court. Resting against a light peach wall are several benches and oversized baskets. Sabeena sits, takes off her sandals, places them into one of the baskets and gestures for us to all do the same. Since very few of us have footwear to remove it is only seconds before we are following her through another set of arches into a second great room.

The front half is more of a parlor/lounge with simple wicker chairs and periwinkle blue tables. The back end is the dining area where two rows of sizeable pillows are lined up the entire width of the building, separated by a series of small mustard yellow tables.

The pillows look soft and inviting. Each is a different color of maroon, gold or brown with complex patterns. Some have smaller throw pillows atop them while others have enormous bolsters. These too are dashing in shades of deep purple and gold.

Bright flora decorates every room, filling the air with sweet scent. Pink potted lotus flowers, yellow roses, deep red and gold marigolds, white jasmine, pale pink orchids, purple bougainvillea and green ferns. It's as if we entered an indoor tropical paradise. Actually, it's the most foliage and color I've seen within the village.

Oddly the walls throughout the building are a muted white and to my right is a long pale pink counter that runs the depth of the room. Behind it stands a small frail man wearing a soft yellow dhoti. His graying hair is neatly combed and his smile is as wide as the mustache upon his kind face.

"Pappu," Sabeena sings, "these are my guests. They will be staying here tonight. We will place them on the rooftop garden. Please see to it that there are enough cushions for them."

"Yes Sabeena," Pappu replies. He bows slightly and nods a small hello, then slips out from behind the counter and disappears through a small door to his right.

"Please rest comfortably," Sabeena says, motioning to the pillows and chairs, "while I prepare some food and drink." She smiles ear to ear then adds an encouraging, "Please -" before exiting through the same door as Pappu.

Not trusting myself to indulge in the comfort of a pillow without the distraction of food to keep me from falling asleep, I head to the nearest chair and sit down next to Dmitry.

"You know, my son, I have been thinking," I start.

"As have I."

"Please – I - I need to finish. I love you Dmitry. You have grown into a noble man. I couldn't ask for a better son. Words cannot express what you have done for me – what you have given me." I gaze from him to Lily and then take my sisters by the hand. "I love you all. I am so blessed to have such a loving, strong, devoted family. Yet the repercussions of our actions have been unbearable and I foresee they will only get worse with time."

"That is why we have to...." Dmitry starts.

"Stop this," I interrupt. "It needs to end before too much damage is done. Right now, you are all unknown - innocent. You can wake up tomorrow and go about your lives, never to be hunted again. Which is how life should be."

"Not for me," Dmitry adds.

"No son, not for you. Which is why tomorrow morning you and I will say our goodbyes and turn ourselves in to the King. Beg his forgiveness and pray for his mercy."

"Mercy? From Theothantanos, never! We will be slaughtered like animals," Dmitry rages.

"Maybe so. That is a risk I am willing to take. I will gladly give my life if it means saving everyone else's!"

"How noble of you to serve yourself up on a platter to that unjust pig of a monarch -" Poppy bellows, "but Dmitry will not be the apple in your mouth or the garnish under your belly. I will not let him go. I have lost everything to that evil monster. First my mother, then my father and now my sister. Your son is all I have left, and he is not for you or for the King or for anyone else but ME!"

Dmitry pulls Poppy into his chest where she falls to pieces once more. Soothingly he consoles her, "I'm not going Poppy, I have a better idea." He gazes to me, "May I?"

I nod in reply.

"We cross over to Earth. Go back to Baltimore!"

"They will still track you. Customs pulled me out of that park seconds after I accidently used my ability," I remind.

"That's because you registered and crossed over legally."

"But...."

"It can be done, Tracy and I have used a homemade portal before. That is how we pulled Lily through. She's not on record, no one knows about her here."

"It's too risky. We could land in the grey."

"You just said you were willing to die!"

"The grey is worse than death!"

"It won't happen."

"We'd be illegal!"

"HAH!" Lily coughs.

"What about us?" Naomi and Naysa ask.

"Go! What's stopping you?"

"But we...."

"Have two heads. You're not the first set of conjoined twins on Earth. And there you won't be forced into a life of exile! There are twins, in case you were going to ask, and blacks, yes there are even black twins. We could all go and we would all fit in. That is IF you want to."

Dmitry pauses to sigh, "Would we have to be careful? Yes, but I don't need to run fast. Not when there's so much public transportation." He smiles then points to Winston and Warwick. "You won't need to move the earth. They have backhoes and tractors for that. Granted you might want to get some new digs, but really you don't have to. Poppy can chew gum to blow a bubble and Tracy, aren't you tired of having fleas?"

"That has NEVER happened!" Tracy defends.

"Never?" Dmitry teases, raising an eyebrow.

Tracy looks to Lily with a terrified expression. "Don't believe him!" he begs. Lily just laughs.

"And Dad, you don't have to heal. They have doctors and hospitals for that – and - and they have... Orvah!"

I wasn't expecting Dmitry of all people to hit that chord, which was well played.

"We can all be together, one big family. What do you say?"

"Oh Dmitry, we want to do it!" Naomi squeals.

"If you go, we go," Warwick adds.

"Lily?" Dmitry questions.

Lily nods in response

"Cool," Tracy adds.

"Dad? What do you say? Will you join us?"

"Well, I don't think I could come up with a better idea myself!"

The most positive energy I have ever seen engulfs us.

Honestly, I can't think of a better alternative at the moment. The thought of being with family, possibly reuniting with Orvah, and getting out of Realm is too exciting.

That evening we feasted on Daal-Baati, Baingan Ka and Lehsuni Daal. It was the most scrumptious food to cross my lips in a long while. Sabeena generously insisted we have the luxury of freshening up in the bathroom facility located in her own suite. After we all had a turn basking in the glory of indoor plumbing she led us up to the rooftop garden where nine cushions were laid out over the grass floor under the starry sky.

The air was much cooler and with a clean body, full belly and the prospect of a better tomorrow we all gratefully crawled upon our beds and turned in. I didn't realize how heavy my eyelids were until my head actually hit the pillow. Within seconds I fell into a deep slumber dreaming about the possibilities....

I see Orvah's face, the gold in her hair and the smile on her lips. When I look back up into her dark eyes they are Sabeena's - her smile - her golden tables - purple pillows and my delicious dinner. I pick up a roll and bite it. It is hard and dry, crumbling in my mouth. I chew and chew and chew in the warm sun. It burns bright, blinding me with its light. I see a shadow and then grey - nothing but grey. I can feel the heat of the day scorching my face, drying my saliva, making it difficult to swallow. It hurts. The roll feels sharp against my throat, like razorblades.

Razorblades.

Razorblades....

I am awakened. A hand is over my mouth, a whisper is in my ear, "Shhhh" - and a razorblade is at my throat.

TRACY

Chapter Fourteen
Gone

"Tracy wake up!"

Ughh, "Leave me alone, I just fell asleep," I grumble

"No you didn't. It's morning and something's happened. I need you to get up!"

Grrr, I growl to myself. A dainty pair of hands presses firmly against my chest, rousing me from my slumber, exciting me with the hopes that it could be Lily. Wiping the sleep from my eyes I open them to see Poppy crouching over me.

My smile quickly fades to a frown.

"Oh, gross! Stop touching me," I whine.

"Shut it moron. The only reason I'm waking you is because Jaasin's missing."

My body reacts before the words even sink in. I jolt upright while asking, "What do you mean Jaasin's missing?" The abrupt action causes my forehead to slam into Poppy's. She loses her balance, topples over backwards, does a shoulder roll and lands on both feet in a crouching position.

"Ouch, quit it," I stupidly grumble while rubbing my forehead, knowing full well it was my fault to begin with.

"Damn it Tracy!" She yells, "You're such a ... whatever – now's not the time! When Dmitry and I awoke, a few others were already out of bed. We went down to the dining area but Jaasin was not there. He seems to be missing, Dmitry's freaking out."

"Where is he now?"

"Running all over town looking for him."

Springing to my feet I thunder down three flights of stairs to the gathering room where Winston, Warwick, Naomi and Nasya are waiting.

"How long have you been up?" I ask.

"My brother and I were the first to awaken. It was still dark so we came down here as to not wake the others. Fifteen minutes later we watched the sun rise from the back garden. Naomi and Nasya joined us about an hour after that."

"What time is it now?"

"Eight fifteen," Naomi responds.

"When did you realize Jaasin was missing?"

"About twenty minutes ago," Nasya adds.

"Only three others were sleeping when we awoke." Poppy assures, "so we came down to find everyone else. Only Jaasin was not here."

"I can't find him anywhere!" Dmitry pants as he sprints in. "I circled the city twice. He's nowhere to be found."

"What about Sabeena? Have you asked her?"

"I haven't, good idea," Dmitry answers then bolts up the stairs.

I can hear him knocking on her door as I run up the stairs two by two. When I hit the second-floor landing Dmitry's raps become a little louder.

"Sabeena?" he whispers through the door. "Sabeena?" As I jog the corridor to her suite his knocking turns into a pound.

"Sabeena?" he calls, "Sabeena! Is my father with you?" When Sabeena does not answer, Dmitry turns the knob and opens the unlocked door.

The room is empty. The bed has been made and all Sabeena's bags and other possessions have been removed. Dmitry's eyes widen.

Wildly he cries, "*You are safe now - nothing to fear. This land here is sacred, the air will protect you, its provisions will heal you – you will see.* I should have known this was a set-up all along!"

"A set-up? Don't jump to conclusions."

"Don't jump to conclusions?"

"Jaasin could be in the shower."

"Again?"

"When was the last time he enjoyed such a luxury?"

"Fine."

Dmitry stomps toward the restroom muttering under his breath.

"He's not here, Tracy," Dmitry yells. Seconds later he is back at my side. "Jaasin's gone, Sabeena is gone. I'm not stupid, I know one plus one is two. She took him, Tracy, I know it!"

"You don't know that, Dmitry. Sabeena's a nice girl. She graciously took us in, gave us food, a nice place to sleep."

"It was just a front, a trap so we would like her – trust her."

"Why? Why would she do such a thing?" I question.

"BECAUSE SHE WORKS FOR THE KING!" Dmitry screams.

"GET AHOLD OF YOURSELF!" I yell back. My temper is starting to flare. I don't want to fight with my best friend but this whole mission is falling apart at the seams, and so are we. Right now his assumptions are so irrational and that's me talkin'!

"GET AHOLD OF MYSELF! GET AHOLD OF MYSELF?" Dmitry rages, "JAASIN IS MISSING AND YOU OBVIOUSLY DON'T CARE!"

"I do care, I just think there has to be a more logical explanation other than Sabeena."

"SHE DID IT – SHE TOOK HIM! YOU CAN'T TELL ME OTHERWISE!" Dmitry roars, stomping his foot.

"What have I done?" Sabeena's voice calls from the threshold of her room.

Dmitry's mouth snaps shut. Childish yes, but I hit him with the old "*I told you so*" smirk. He retaliates by shooting me a look that totally implies "*keep it up and I'm gonna deck you!*"

"Well, are you going to tell me what I've done or not?" Sabeena questions yet again. When neither Dmitry or I respond she scolds, "I could hear the two of you shouting from outside. You have awoken and distressed all my guests. Not only that but you have come to call on me and entered into MY suite without permission! What do you have to say for yourselves?"

"My father is missing."

"And you think I took him?"

"No – I mean, yes," Dmitry blunders.

"Perhaps he went for a walk."

"Where were you?"

"Not that it's any of your business, but I was packing the camels for the journey home today."

Sabeena points to the balcony where below a small herd of camels is tied together, draped with blankets and baskets full of goods.

"I searched the village, he is not out for a walk."

"Searched the village? It is quite large."

"Twice!"

"I see. You had enough time to search the village – twice – and yet you did not see me right out front with four camels? Perhaps you missed him."

"I wasn't searching for you."

"But if I took him, shouldn't you have been?"

Dmitry hisses in frustration and I decide to step in before he has to put his foot in his mouth a second time.

"I apologize for my friend. We have been through a lot in the last few days. It's a long story, one you would have to know to understand. The point is, Dmitry's father is an extremely important man. When we woke up and he was not there, he panicked – we all did. I am sorry for the inconveniences we have caused you – and for barging into your room."

"Perhaps he is still sleeping, your friend just didn't see!"

Oohhh, I'm not sure if she understands how cranky Dmitry is right now. Rubbing his mistakes in his face is not a good thing to do. However, I am completely mistaken when Dmitry smiles a sarcastic little smile and responds with, "You're right, Sabeena. How about we all check together – then you will see?"

"After you," she responds, stepping away from the doorway.

Winston, Warwick, Naomi, Nasya and Poppy are all waiting outside in the hall along with three awakened guests from the other rooms on the second floor. On our way through the corridor Sabeena politely takes each guest aside and whispers her sincerest apologies, followed by an offer for a free meal downstairs. Dmitry turns left into the stairwell and ambles up two flights to the rooftop garden with the lot of us in tow.

Once there he slams the door open, startling Lily, who had still been sleeping. All the other cushions are empty except one other.

"What's going on?" Lily asks while springing to her feet.

Ignoring Lily, Dmitry addresses Sabeena, "See, only two others!"

"I see how it would appear so."

"Appear?"

"Appear was the word."

Wow, she's really giving it to Dmitry. He's trying to keep his cool but I know by the clench of his jaw and the look in his eyes that he's about to unhinge. Somehow this makes me like Sabeena even more! Ahh, with all this intensity it's nice to find something that will give me the S and G's I crave!

"Don't you think it funny - that in one-hundred-degree heat - the portliest of your crew would require a blanket to cover his girth while sleeping?"

All eyes shift to the large mass covered by a heavy wool blanket. Dmitry walks over, gently taps it with his toe, then frantically rips the blanket up revealing several pillows lined up to form the shape of a large body.

"Kirill!" he seethes.

"We should have known," Poppy adds, "Without Alia's ability to restrain him...." She bends her head. Unable to continue, she starts to weep.

"Restrain? He was a friend of yours, was he not?" Sabeena questions.

"No," Dmitry growls, "No he was not. You're right Poppy, I should have seen this coming."

"Looks like you owe me an apology."

"And you'll get one if you ever shut that sassy mouth of

yours!" Dmitry snaps.

"I take you in and this is how you thank me?" Sabeena retaliates, "So obtuse – no wonder you have had so much misfortune!"

Dmitry snaps his head toward her. His stance, the look in his eyes and the heavy breathing all indicate he's about to go bananas.

"You know what?" he yells, "you're right!"

Wow! Wasn't expecting that.

"We're done!" Dmitry continues. "I'm sorry Sabeena. I would like to explain my actions to you but I will not invite any more trouble your way. The less you know the better. You are a kind soul, I thank you for the nourishment and shelter."

Dmitry turns, gazes into my eyes then walks over to Poppy, who is still weeping. Softly he takes her into his arms. Caressing her gently he kisses the top of her head, "My love, it's time for you to go home."

"What?" Poppy squeaks. Pulling away she looks up to Dmitry. Her eyes are puffy and bloodshot.

"Winston? Warwick? Please take her back to the cottage with my aunts."

"Dmitry?" Naomi questions.

"No more."

"But?"

"It's over – go home."

"Okay," Naomi whispers.

"Lily, you too."

"What? What's going on?" Lily cries.

"Tracy, see to it that Lily gets back safely - to HER home. Understand?"

I nod.

"What are you talking about? Why won't you tell me what's going on?"

"Father is gone. Kirill has taken him. Your part in this mission is over. It was over a long time ago, only I refused to believe it. The time has come for you to go back to where you came from."

"No!" Lily shouts. Her cheeks begin to flush. "I'm not going anywhere!"

"Damn it Lily, do as you're told for once!"

"What is it with you ordering everyone around?"

"I'm your brother!"

"He's my father – he needs us!"

"There is nothing you can do for him."

"Says you!"

Lily's skin begins to lose color. I've only seen this happen when she's been startled. Somehow today her anger is enough to do the trick and she fades before our eyes. Dmitry grabs her wrist before she completely disappears.

"Ouch! Stop it, Dmitry. I'm tired of you getting physical every time we have a disagreement."

"I have no other choice."

"You do! You always do!"

"You're dangerous Lily, you don't belong here."

"Me? Dangerous? The last time you grabbed me like this you slit my wrist. Now what are you going to do?"

"You can't control your ability. Look at yourself! How am I supposed to protect you?"

"I don't need your protection!" Lily yells.

Dmitry howls in pain then falls forward onto his knees clutching his abdomen. In between labored breaths he swears.

"Dmitry!" Poppy cries. Kneeling beside him she places one hand upon his shoulder. The other caresses his back. "Are you alright?"

"Do I look alright?" he snaps. Hastily he pulls himself out from under her touch and stands. "Go home Poppy," he orders, then dashes through the door.

Crap!

Without wasting another minute, I transform into a Peregrine Falcon and take off into the morning sky. A rush of air catches my eye about two miles off and I know without a doubt it's Dmitry. Lucky for me the combination of exhaustion and

Lily's punch to the gut has him running at a much slower pace. It takes me two minutes to cover the distance. When I see him and not just his wake of dust I dive toward the ground, transform into a clouded leopard and charge.

My feet pound the dry soil until I'm directly behind him. In one swift move I pounce, knock him forward and watch as he tumbles. Prowling swiftly, I follow as his body rolls six times before stopping. Quickly I leap onto his chest and pin him to the ground.

His face is torn, his lip bloody and his breathing is extremely labored. Still he looks at me with intense eyes. I stare into them. Swim in the vast aqua marine pools, wondering if he knows it's me upon his chest. Slowly I lower my snout until it is inches from his face.

I am so angry with him. Mad for the way this has all turned out. And even though our series of misfortunes has not been his fault, per se, he's the one responsible for leading us down this path.

Hungrily I watch his eyes dilate. I can smell his sweat - taste his fear. I open my jaw to expose my razor-sharp fangs. Dmitry's body is still, the jugular vein in his throat throbs; he swallows hard then closes his eyes.

If he weren't so insistent upon freeing Jaasin, Alia would not be gone.

WHYYY!!! - I Roar.

On the other hand, I never would have met Lily – sweet, sweet Lily. Slowly I close my mouth, transform back into my own self and wait for Dmitry to look at me. His body stirs after sensing the shift in weight that's pinning him down. His eyes open.

"Get off!" he whispers.

"No!"

I want an apology, yet his baby blues have already given me one. I want this to all be over, yet I know the worst has just begun. And most of all, I want Alia back - but that is something Dmitry cannot give me.

"Get off," he begs.

"You will run."

"I – I can't breathe."

"If you take off running I will transform into an elephant and see to it that what you say is true – understand?"

When he shakes his head I slowly roll off onto the ground. For two minutes I lie there beside him, gazing up into the sky. Finally, when I think Dmitry has regained his breath I ask, "What are you doing?"

"I'm going to find him, Tracy."

"Alone."

"Just like the first time."

"I was with you then."

"I know."

"I'm with you now."

"I know."

"They could have about eight to ten hours on you."

"That's not an issue, you know that."

"He could be anywhere."

"True."

Sighing, Dmitry climbs up onto his feet and holds out a hand for me to take. He brushes the dust off his clothing then makes eye contact.

"So where were you headed?" I ask.

"To the one place he is bound to turn up."

I look at my friend questioningly.

"The King's castle – with or without you."

Chapter Fifteen
Decisions

I'm tired and my feet hurt from walking. Today's jaunts as a falcon and leopard were the third and fourth transformations since I changed into that Chirachnophagous. Wicked-ass animal! What an episode that was. I should have known turning into something that close to death would kill me. I shake my head at the notion.

Life, how sweet it is - and yet, how bitter. I've been thinking a lot lately. About women - yes, I'll always think about women, but mostly I've been thinking about life. Dmitry and I, our adventures have always been precarious.

Kirill said that without risk there is no reward. It was his reasoning for hiring some muscle, following us to Jaasin's cage and plunging a knife into Poppy's back. He thought by taking the situation into his own hands, rather than just informing the King of our plan, he would earn a hefty pay-off and more.

And although I am angry that Kirill's quest for a decorated honor from His Majesty involved an attempt to kill our team, I don't disagree with his initial thought ... without risk there is no reward. It is, after all, the motif for our crusade.

Not until this morning had I thought about my reward, what I wanted to gain from all this risk. Dmitry's is easy. He wants his father and he's not going to stop until he gets him.

I get that. I couldn't imagine life without my dad. Sure, he was a young punk when he had me, but he was always there for me and every day with him was ... well - fun! I want that for Dmitry and I'll do anything to help him get it.

But there comes a time when you have to level with yourself. I could continue on this journey with my friend and chance losing my life to reunite him with his father. It's a sad scenario that I voluntarily signed up for just hours earlier. I was ready to die in order to save Dmitry, because I knew if I didn't demand to stay behind, he would have been the one to relinquish his own life. And I know that if I continue on this journey with him, I would do it again in a heartbeat.

But what would my old man do without me? What good is it uniting one, only to divide another? What will Poppy do now without her sister?

These thoughts have been haunting me since we emerged from that cave without Alia. This expedition has always been dangerous but I never actually thought of it as life-threatening before (even after that day on Lachlan's boat). Now reality has taken its toll and let's face it, it's time to get serious. Jaasin will never be a free man. Not as long as the King lives. And he has been living for two hundred and seventy-three years.

My friend will fail and if he's fortunate enough to leave those grounds in one piece he will still have a family to come home to. He'll have Poppy, Naomi and Nasya. And with my help he'll have his sister. He will have Lily.

The girl I fell hard for the second I looked at her beautiful face. I knew that day at Revitalize and I know now that I want HER. I want Lily to be my reward – to be my girl, one day my wife and then the mother of my children. I want to be a father, loved unconditionally by my son. Just like the love I feel for my dad and just like the feelings Dmitry has for Jaasin.

Becoming the dragon breathed the fire right back into my soul and escaping my self-proclaimed death sentence gave me the insight I needed to make my decision today.

It wasn't easy telling Dmitry that I wasn't going to join him. Yet deep down I think he knew it all along. Just as I knew, by the way he called it quits on the rooftop, this fork in the road was meant for him and him alone. So, I vowed to take Lily under my wing and protect her for as long as I live.

Dmitry took off before I could say goodbye and part of me was grateful for that. I was able to interpret his departing as a *see you later buddy*, which is all I really wanted to hear from him anyway.

Still my heart is heavy as I walk back to the village, moping through its streets until I stumble upon a large lake. The pool of water is magnificent with fifty-two ghats leading down to its glassy surface. Gazing around I see each stairwell is empty except for one.

Directly across the way in front of a large temple is Sabeena who's sitting cross-legged on the top step facing the water with her eyes closed. Below her stands a man with short dark hair dressed in an ornate bright white sherwani coat.

With the House of God at her back, her meditating pose and the man's attire, I assume Sabeena is praying to a man of faith. It would be rude to interrupt, so I decide to return to the guesthouse instead. There I find Nasya, Naomi, Winston, Warwick and Poppy still waiting for our return on the rooftop.

"Did you find him?" Poppy asks. Her voice is meek and her appearance timid. She has lowered her shield, exposing her vulnerability, which is a very rare thing for Poppy to do.

I nod in response.

"Then why is he not with you?"

"Poppy," I whisper. "You know why."

I watch her expression change from nervous to livid as she stares through me - and I wait for it. Any second she's going to unleash a world of fury upon me. I'm ready. I knew it was par for the course. It's what she does.

Bring it on Poppy. I know it's in there.

And before the thought is out of my mind she's screaming, "WHY DID YOU LET HIM GO? WHY DIDN'T YOU STOP HIM?"

Her hands slap my face and beat against my chest. Not once do I fight back. Though I must admit, one day I would really like to dish it back to her. But I know today is not the day; she's not strong enough. She hasn't been since Kirill cut her and she won't be for a long time to come. Not with the newest of scars burrowed into her soul. Not with Dmitry gone.

I stand here posing as her punching bag. Willing her to strike me until the pain within has subsided. Each blow grows softer and softer until both of her hands stop over my heart. Slowly she slides her arms around the sides of my torso to my back then buries her head into my chest and cries.

"Oh Poppy -" Is all I manage to squeak out before a flood of tears falls from my eyes. I grab her tight, cradle her against me, and weep. I shed tears for my best friend, who has chosen to jump from the frying pan into the fire, plead for his safe return and mourn for my littlest friend, who has left me forever. It feels good to let it all out - really let go. It's the only time I have allowed myself to grieve since we found out the news.

Dmitry - Alia, what will I... what will we do without you?

Impulsively I grab Poppy's face into my hands, pull her up to mine and kiss her softly on the forehead. Immediately she stifles her sniffling, her body goes limp; she pulls back and gazes up at me. Her eyes brimming with tears, she looks at me in horror. I swallow hard, preparing myself for another beating. What in the world could have willed me to do such a thing?

"Gross!" Poppy whispers. Her tone is honest yet playful and I am completely caught off guard.

What is this? I question to myself.

"I'm the one person you said you'd never kiss – what's wrong with you?" she razzes.

This is so unlike her I just don't even know what to say. Her tears turn to laughter and before I know it a half-assed apology chuckles out.

"I have no idea! But it was so disgusting I'll never do it again."

"Promise?" She smiles.

"Promise."

Poppy places her head back onto my chest. It feels good to hug a woman who's usually as cold as ice and our embrace lasts a good five minutes until finally she lets go. Straightening her yellow sundress, she clears her throat then says, "Well, I suppose we should go home now."

I just nod, unsure of how to tell Poppy that I'm not going with her. Not without Lily, that is.

"Sabeena left us some provisions for the trip. Then she went to look for Lily."

"I passed her on my way back. She was just meditating on

some steps. Lily wasn't with her."

Grabbing a rucksack off the floor Poppy adds, "Guess we'll leave you to it then."

Again I nod, grateful for her astute awareness of the situation.

I study the five of them standing before me, searching for just the right words. Winston and Warwick's dark tattooed faces are so strong and unmoved while Naomi and Nasya's appear softer, frailer. All four of them are still wearing the same threadbare attire from the day we rescued Jaasin.

Then there is Poppy, whose summer frock is as bright as the midday sun. It seems so out of place and I wonder why she chose it. But I suppose the day she changed into it inside the cave everything seemed so radiant, especially after our swim. Or maybe there wasn't much of a selection in the bag Alia had packed; either way its bright yellow glow doesn't fit in with our downfall and I find myself despising the dress and wishing she would leave so I wouldn't have to look at it any longer. So I wouldn't have to remember happier times while thinking about impending doom.

I refocus my attention on the bag of supplies that Poppy has slung over her shoulder. I hadn't noticed it upon my arrival but now I see each one of them has a sack of their own. Three extra rucksacks lean against the building by the door. Again, I find I have nothing to say.

Apparently neither does Poppy. She nods her farewell then slides through the threshold disappearing into the dark stairwell. Winston and Warwick follow immediately without any form of valediction. Their actions, or lack thereof, sting but I know deep down it's their way of telling me this is not a permanent parting. Naomi and Nasya, on the other hand, give me a quick squeeze before joining the others.

It is a fleeting goodbye that leaves me standing alone on the rooftop garden with the extra haversacks. I look at the bags, thinking about how nice it would be if we were all going home together, then sigh. Slowly I climb up onto a stone pillar to sit and stew. The perch gives me an unobstructed view, allowing me to watch my friends make their way to the edge of the city and out into the golden meadow beyond. There Poppy stops and turns back, her hair glistening in the sun as she waves her final adieu.

When they are nothing more than a speck on the horizon I take the opportunity to stand and gaze around for Lily. I find there are too many hiding areas concealed by buildings and temples, so I decide to transform into a falcon once more, which gives me the ability to cover more ground in less time.

The city is spectacular. I make my way back to the water in search of Sabeena, only to find she is no longer there. Neither is the man that was standing before her, and an eerie sensation begins to ruffle my feathers. It strikes me as odd that no one is at the lake, considering how hot it is. Not even an animal drinks or bird swims across its surface. Curious? Yes ... but I am far more interested in finding Lily's whereabouts.

I take off flying down every road, every alleyway to no avail. Surely Lily would be visible by now; a lot of time has passed since she argued with Dmitry. Granted she did disappear for a long while after witnessing Scylla and Charybdis, but today it's been several hours. Time is ticking away and I am worried I might lose my opportunity to find her. Then it hits me! I know what I have to do.

Quickly I soar through the air back to Sabeena's garden. Before my feet hit the ground, I roll into a cyclone and emerge as a golden retriever. The second my paws make contact with the grassy ground I bound over to Lily's cushion and bury my nose in it, inhaling her sweet smell.

I may not be the kind of tracker that Kirill is, but I should be able to follow her scent. Off I go, down all three flights of stairs, out through the open court and back into the market.

YIKES! The spices burn my nostrils. The aroma is so overwhelming it brings tears to my eyes. Luckily enough with my snout tight to the ground I can still make out Lily's scent. It leads me back toward the spot where Dmitry collapsed after she and I had entered the village.

Then she turned back, circled through another row of buildings and out into the center of town, past the large temple and down toward the ghats where I saw Sabeena earlier. There I pick up two other scents. One is a deep musk, the other a daintier spice.

I follow all three up toward the entrance of the temple. There they split. The musk enters the building whereas the other two turn, leading me back to the front of the guesthouse where they fuse with yet another, extremely pungent, overly appalling stench.

I track the stink through the other side of the village out to where the dirt ground turns back into another golden grassy plain. Off in the distance lay rows of green lush mountain. I spring through the tall grass then take off into a sprint when I see four camels in the distance. As I close in on them, I spy Sabeena riding atop one of the camels. I stop to squint. The three other animals are packed with parcels. Sabeena is riding alone and I begin to worry. How stupid of me to assume Lily would be with them. Why did I follow the pervasive fetor instead of her delicate body odor?

Then I see it, a slight silhouette peeking out from in front of the humped beasts. Walking with them in her white eyelet baby-doll dress is Lily!

Inane? Yes, but I don't want Lily to see me this way. Especially after Dmitry's flea accusations. Which only happened once by the way! Anywho, quickly I change back into my handsome old self and stride off calling out her name.

"Lily! – Lily!"

She stops and turns. Placing her hand above her brow to shield the sun she squints in my direction.

"Lily!" I call.

"Tracy?" she questions.

I take off, running to her at the sound of my name.

"Tracy!" she excitedly acknowledges, then sprints toward me.

Together we collide into a warm embrace.

"It is you!" she chuckles, "You came back!"

"Back? I'm not the one that left."

"But when I returned to the guesthouse you were all gone. I didn't know what to do."

"I told you Lily, no matter what happens, I'll protect you."

Her eyebrows crinkle and her lips smile.

"Oh Tracy!"

It feels so good being back in Lily's company, especially without the crew. Yet we are not alone and somehow Sabeena has convinced Lily to accompany her home, so here we are walking hand in hand toward Sabeena's farm. Her father Baneet and her mother Toya are out front awaiting Sabeena's arrival.

They graciously welcome Lily and me with open arms and kindly introduce us to their three sons. The eldest, Salil, is twenty-five years of age while Virochan and Viraaj, the ten-year-old twins, are the youngest out of all eight of their children.

In between the boys are five daughters. Aarai is the eldest of the girls at age twenty-three, Damyani is age sixteen, Champa age fifteen, and then there is Tabassum who is twelve. Of course, we know Sabeena, who like Lily is nineteen years of age. Each one of Sabeena's sisters is just as pretty as she.

We then tour their crops of pearl millet, mung bean, guar, ground nuts and sorghum. The plants are lush and plentiful. Their farmland is impressively vast and that night we feast on the most amazing delicacies under a large arbor in the back yard.

Baneet and Toya's house is majestic with an open floor plan that boasts a comfortable kitchen, dining and family room in the main living area. There are plenty of windows that allow light to filter in for the many flowering plants that climb the walls and furniture.

It is a single story decorated in earthy tones with accent colors to match the flora inside and out. There is a large covered porch in the front with many chairs for relaxation and five good-sized bedrooms. When it is time for bed they pair Lily with Sabeena and Aarai for the night, giving me the only guest room.

My stomach is full and my body is tired but still I find it hard to sleep. I lie awake tossing and turning in a stranger's bed suddenly aware of how lonely I feel without my friends. I am lost in thought when the door to my room suddenly creaks open. Straining my eyes against the dark I see no one there. It's a completely ridiculous notion but I swear I'm not alone.

"Lily?" I whisper, "Is that you?"

"Did I wake you?" she responds.

"No."

"Sorry to barge in, I can't sleep."

"Neither can I."

I pat the bed, hoping she will join me. Seconds later the bed dips and I feel her warmth sliding in next to me.

"I can't see you."

"I didn't want to be caught." Lily's breath exhales excitedly then she adds, "It's the first time I've used my ability when I actually wanted to."

"Good. Pretty soon you'll be able to will it whenever you want. You just need to practice."

"Can you teach me how?"

"Sure." After a moment I add, "I'd really like to see your face."

"Okay."

There is a long pause while nothing happens. "Tracy?" Lily questions.

"Yes."

"What should I do?"

"You should want to show me – and you will," I whisper. Patiently I wait while seconds turn to minutes. Within two, Lily begins to materialize.

"There you are!"

She smiles.

"Lily?"

"Yes?"

"Where'd you go today?"

"I – I was going to leave, I went as far as the meadow but I got scared. Then I went down by the water. I'm just so darn mad. Not just with Dmitry. It seems lately I'm angry about everything. I'm scared and, and most of all I think I'm mostly sad. Tracy I – I'm so lost, I just don't know what to do."

"Me either."

Softly I pull her into my arms. We lie pressed together, her head nestled in the crook of my arm with my chin resting on top of her head. I glide my fingers over her moist skin, gently stroking her arm up and down, up and down. The methodical movement clears my mind and I begin to relax tucked up in Lily's warmth. My eyes are about to close when she breaks the silence with her soft sweet voice.

"How did you find me?

"That's for me to know and for you to never find out!" I whisper in her ear. My lips feel the heat radiating off the snug supple skin behind her neck.

She pokes my ribs then demands, "Tell me."

"No."

"Come on."

"Fine, I tracked you."

"Duh, how?"

"You really want to know?"

"Yes!"

"Your scent."

Lily looks up. Her blue eyes lock on mine then she crinkles her nose.

"Yuck!"

"What? You smell good."

"It's one hundred degrees outside, I highly doubt it."

I can't help but chuckle.

"What?"

"You're so cynical at times, Lily. Trust me, a woman

doesn't have to be freshly showered and wear perfume to smell good. The way you are now – natural – perspiring – it drives me crazy."

I grab the side of her waist with my free hand and give it a little squeeze as I nuzzle my face into the crook of her neck. I inhale then groan with pleasure. This is what she does to me.

Swiftly she jabs me in the side again. Disappointed, I let go of her and roll back onto the pillow.

"Cut it out! And there's no way you could track my scent ... unless?"

"What?" I question.

Lily props herself up onto her elbow to look down at me. Her eyes are wild with recrimination.

"You became the dog again, didn't you?"

"No," I quickly deny.

"Don't lie to me. You totally did – I can see it in that mischievous smirk you've got played out across your face."

"Woof!" I bark teasingly.

Lily cracks up laughing, "You animal!"

"You have no idea!" I say provokingly then bark again causing her to laugh even harder.

"Shhh, you'll wake everyone up!" I reprimand.

Lily buries her head into my naked chest, suppressing her uncontrollable giggling until it subsides. After a minute she repositions her face, laying her cheek against my torso.

"Seriously, Tracy, what are we going to do?" she asks.

Running my fingers through her hair, I sigh, "I wish I had all the answers for you Lily. But what I do know is – even though we've been welcomed here it doesn't mean we belong. I don't think it's right to stay," I add.

Lily nods against my chest.

"Where will we go?"

"I want to take you home."

Promptly she sits up, protesting with a stern, "No!"

"Relax silly, I want to take you to my home. All this time spent rescuing your father makes me miss mine terribly."

Comforted by my explanation, Lily lies back down, placing her head onto my chest once again.

"Can I take you?" I ask.

Unexpectedly she kisses my breastbone. Her soft, warm touch sends a wave of warmth through me, arousing each and every nerve ending. My body tingles, springing to life. I inhale rapidly, craving her more than ever before. My free hand caresses her stomach then brushes up alongside her breast.

Swiftly I pull her up and under me, kissing her mouth most urgently. She returns my fervor, giving in to my every move. Her supple lips part as I gently kiss her throat and when we connect like two pieces of a puzzle she whispers one word into the hot night air.

"Yes!"

Chapter Sixteen
To Flourish a Flower

I wake late in the morning with a smile upon my face. The way the sun hangs in the sky tells me more than half the day has passed. For the first time in days I feel well rested but my body is weak. My stomach grumbles for food and my mouth is dry, exceptionally dry. Not until this moment have I noticed how dehydrated I have become.   Quickly I slide into my trousers then pull on a grey t-shirt. I fling my bag over my shoulder and stumble to the door, pausing momentarily to look back at the room and smile before exiting.

Padding my way through the house I find all is quiet except for the clinking of dishes and a dainty pitter-patter, which appear to be emanating from the kitchen. An inviting spicy aroma greets my nose halfway down the hall, causing my mouth to salivate and my pace to quicken.

"Good afternoon my friend. Did you sleep well?" Sabeena's mother asks as I enter the kitchen.

"Very well thank you," I blushingly reply.

"Hungry dear?"

I nod.

Swiftly Toya shuffles over to me with a mustard yellow dish in her hands. Before I know it, she forces the warm plate into my left hand then grabs me tightly around my right arm just above the wrist. The brisk movement causes the rucksack to slide down off my shoulder and land in the crook of my elbow. Toya pulls the strap from the center of my forearm and slides it to the floor, all the while inspecting my limb most curiously.

Her eyes widen when she looks from the palm of my hand up into my face. Before I know it, she's rolling one of her soft brown thumbs over my dry parted lips. Toya's eyes narrow and she frowns.

"My boy, you are dried out!"

Her mouth purses as she makes a sharp tsk-tsk noise with her teeth and tongue. She releases my hand and scurries across the room. In seconds she is back before me with a large empty glass in her hands. She takes the plate and sets it down upon a wooden island, pushes the goblet into my hold, then cradles her hands around mine. Water begins to rise within the glass. When it is full she looks to me with a stern motherly look.

"There, drink up!" she demands.

Three times she fills my glass with cool crisp water before returning the plate to my hands.

"Good, now take this outside and sit."

I do as I am told and saunter off through the large doors out into the hot midday sun. Waiting outside under the flowery arbor is a large table covered with a decadent spread of food.

"I was just about to call everyone for lunch when you stepped in. Please start; we've all had breakfast. No one will mind."

It is very kind of her but waiting for the family to join us is the least I can do. Sitting back I take another sip of water, though this time it doesn't taste as refreshing. My stomach lurches a wee bit and I'm suddenly stricken with an unwelcoming queasiness.

Toya raises an eyebrow, "Go on now - I insist!" she orders, motioning toward the multiple dishes before me. My belly groans a large bubbling gurgle, encouraging me to give in. I take a pesarattu, most likely left over from breakfast, and half a dozen Khoya dumplings. There is a reddish orange meat dish, which looks scrumptious and smells hot. And I don't mean the temperature kind of hot! I'm pretty sure I have enough water in my gut to put out a small fire but with the thought of burning chilies wreaking havoc on my digestive system, I don't dare.

Toya rings a cowbell as I scoop two helpings of curry onto my plate followed by a small bowl of lentil soup. Minutes later Baneet and his three boys appear far out in the field with Sabeena and Lily in tow.

Lily looks absolutely radiant dressed in a midriff lavender top with cap sleeves and a berry-stained skirt to match her lips. Her hair has been parted down the center and braided on both sides, which interlace at the base of her neck and coil around into a small bun. Pinned above the bun is a lavender rhododendron flower. Honestly the sight of Lily on any given day takes my breath away, but today she's a goddess.

Sometime in the night I felt her creep out of bed and tip-toe back to her room. And though I yearn for her to spend an eternity wrapped up in my arms it was essential, as guests in this house, that she make her way back to Sabeena's room unnoticed. Greeting her now with a kiss would be unfitting, so when she arrives at the table I merely stand.

Stand and lose my cool that is. Completely befuddled I smile an awkward toothy grin and guffaw like some teenage nimrod that was just about to speak to a girl for the first time! Can you believe it? Me of all people!

My heart is racing and my mind is screaming at me to say something, do something besides stand there, so what do I do? I hold out my hand to shake hello, realize how completely absurd my action is, then recoil so quickly I look like I'm having some kind of muscle spasm. In an attempt to cover my blunder, I run my sweaty palm through my hair and yet again let off another giddy chuckle.

"Glad you finally decided to join us, Tracy. I take it you slept well," Lily sings. She's as cool as a cucumber.

It was the best night of my life, thank you.

I attempt to reply with some smooth wordplay but all that comes forth is a pitchy squeak and squawk.

What the what? I scream internally.

Lily smiles and takes a seat across from me. Sabeena rolls her eyes then plops down next to Lily. That's it! I've completely lost my swagger. Disenchanted, I slump back down into my chair as Sabeena's four other sisters materialize from somewhere on the other side of the house.

The table is full of noise and chatter. Baneet and Toya are discussing the upcoming rainstorm, the twins are taking turns flicking each other under the table in between bites of curry and Tabassum, Champa and Damyani are intermittently giggling about something.

I gaze up from my lentil soup to watch Lily eat her second Imarti dessert. She beams at me and when I return her smile a squirt of broth escapes my mouth and dribbles down my chin, causing the three girls to erupt into a fresh bout of laughter.

Quickly I wipe my chin, throw my napkin down on the plate and leave the table. I run through the house, out into the front yard and stand in the middle of the tall golden grass gazing at the mountains beyond.

I am a complete mess!

Where have I gone? I wonder. *What could have done this to me?*

"You're in love!" A velvety voice responds.

Startled, I jump. With my heart in my throat I turn to see Sabeena standing behind me.

"I didn't mean to frighten you."

"It's okay."

"Are you?" She smiles.

Yes, I nod.

"You're very sweet you know? My sisters, they think you are most handsome. That is why they giggle at you. You know how young girls can be."

"Do I?" I question.

"Sit, let's talk."

Together Sabeena and I sit down, allowing the tall grass to envelop us.

"You are ready to leave?"

"Yes."

"To go back home."

Again I nod.

"You could stay as long as you want, you know?"

"Thank you. That's very kind but I wouldn't want to impose."

"You're not."

"It just feels like it."

"I understand. Later I will take you by camel back into the village. There we will fly you home."

"On what?"

"That depends."

"On?"

"What you are comfortable with."

"Okay."

"But before we do, I have some advice for you."

"Okay."

Sabeena holds out her hand, palm facing up. In it she places a seed.

"Relationships are like this seed. It needs water and sun. Together they will make it blossom."

Sabeena then touches the seed with her fingertip. Slowly it begins to sprout, then flower.

"Too much sun and it will wither – too much water and it will drown. No water or sun and it will not flourish."

She hands me a beautiful pink lotus, then stands. I scramble to my feet after her.

"What do you mean?"

"I mean you are the sun. You shine bright for all to see. But it is not good enough - you need water!"

"Water?"

"Water."

I need water?

"But I already had some - a lot actually. Your mom had me drink four glasses so far. How much more do I need?"

Sabeena laughs, "Silly man." She snickers then walks off.

I flop back down feeling defeated. Lying hidden in the tall grass I watch a group of grey clouds roll in. The air is thick with humidity, so much so that you can feel the moisture – smell the rain. My mind ponders over Sabeena's brain-teaser long after she has gone. I may be a pretty boy but I'm not stupid. Normally I'm quick-witted and in the know but today my brain is foggy and drugged.

I close my eyes trying to black everything out, hoping it will help my concentration, but instead I doze off into a hearty power nap. Reawakening I find the sun far off to the west hidden behind a thick dark patch of sky. Springing to my feet, I grab the lotus and head back to the house.

The girls are gathered in Sabeena's room doting over Lily. She now has an ice-blue teardrop jewel encrusted in gold dangling down from the center of her part onto the middle of her forehead. Matching earrings hang down halfway to her shoulders and her makeup has been done. Both hands are covered in henna tattoos and her nails are freshly painted.

More cooing and giggling erupts after I step into the room. Sabeena shoos her sisters out then follows, leaving Lily and I alone for the first time since last night. I walk over to her, mesmerized.

"You look beautiful." I declare.

"You found your voice!" she teases.

"Funny."

"I thought so."

"I couldn't help it. You - you take my breath away."

Lily flushes. Changing the subject she asks, "Where have you been all day? I thought we were leaving."

"We are. I'm sorry for the delay - I fell asleep in the yard."

"But you already slept half the day away!"

I walk to Lily, closing my body in on hers until we are practically touching.

"I know," I whisper into her ear. "It's just that I didn't get much sleep last night!" Flashing a naughty grin, I begin to feel like my old self again. Lily's cheeks turn a brighter shade of pink and I chuckle.

Her hands grab the front of my shirt just under the navel. Balling them into fists, she tugs me into her. Our eyes lock and my breath shallows. Gently I caress the side of her face then slide my fingers over her chin, down her throat and back behind her neck. Running my palm over her beaded sweat, my fingers extend up into her hairline where I cup the back of her head and pull her mouth onto mine. My kiss is deep and full of want.

Suddenly the clearing of a throat by the doorway pulls us apart. "Sorry to interrupt," Sabeena apologizes. "But the storm is nearing. We should go unless you intend to stay another night."

It is nearly nightfall as we make our way back into the village. Sabeena leads us around the lake to the large white temple, where she stops. Climbing down from her camel, she beckons Lily and I to follow. Together we scale the stairs and are greeted under the ornate archway by a man, the same man that stood on the stairs while Sabeena was meditating the day before.

"Greetings my children."

"Janardan," Sabeena greets him.

The man bows to her.

"You remember my friend Lily?"

Janardan smiles kindly and nods his head, "It is nice to be seeing you," he adds.

"My other friend Tracy."

Again, he smiles and nods.

"I have been expecting you. Please come in."

We follow Janardan through the main portion of the temple to the back door where he leads us out into the night and under a large marble and stone slab mandapa. It's a rich royal blue with columns that have gold and teal accents with an intricate red pinnacle roof. The pavilion is decorated in a bird motif with a large mahogany table at its center surrounded by several oversized pillows.

Dozens of carpets, mats and dhurries of various colors and patterns are strewn across the floor overlapping one another. More are rolled and stacked in corners against dark shelves full of jewel-encrusted goblets, Diwali lanterns and brass Jinn lamps.

Janardan motions for us all to take a seat then kneels down upon a yellow and gold cushion. Before him is a round silver bowl full of burning stones, an old book, a large scroll, five urns and several small dishes full of brightly colored powders. He gazes at Lily then begins to speak.

"This temple was created in your world over two thousand years ago for the Hindu God Brahma. Though here in Realm, he was no different than you and I. He too had an ability and with it he created the lake. It and this temple are two of the many things that unite our lands, though in each world they signify different meanings and wield different powers. I understand in India the lake is known for its healing powers, but here in Realm, the story of the lake is a story of love, not revenge, and its powers are so much more."

"So I've been told," Lily responds.

"So, you have my child, so you have!" The man chuckles. "My name is Janardan. It means one who helps people, so how may I help you tonight?"

"My friends wish to go back home," Sabeena answers.

"To Earth?"

"No," I interrupt. "To my home. It's over four thousand miles to the west by flight."

"Far too long to walk."

"Yes," I confirm.

"I see. There are a few options for you. A Garuda for one."

"Okay," Lily agrees.

"What else?" I question.

"A Rukh?"

"Better. Is there anything else?"

"But of course!" Janardan smiles. After an uncomfortable silence he continues, "Did you know I am a direct descendent of Brahma?"

Both Lily and I shake our heads no.

"My family has watched over this village for centuries. Mythological folklore on Earth tells a story about how Brahma's wife Saraswati placed a curse over him and this land."

Janardan pauses to flip through the old book, seemingly searching for something.

"Ah, yes, here it is. It says here that her spell wouldn't allow Brahma to be worshiped as a God, but later she reduced the curse, permitting his praise here in what is known as the Town of Pushkar on Earth."

Janardan closes the book and stands.

"But in truth, her spell was a protective enchantment - one that still encapsulates this village today! You see Saraswati had a brother born with the head of an elephant. And several of both her and Brahma's descendants were without talent - including two of his very own sons.

"In those years, Realm was ruled by an evil man named Styrrgunnar. Much like our King today, he despised those with deformities and without power. He formed an army and set out to destroy them. - Funny how history repeats itself! – Anyway, back then Brahma was busy creating a beautiful village for his people. A city nestled far away in a valley surrounded by mountains. It was a place of knowledge where anyone could come to learn about music, art and science.

"The King found out about the land and set forth to massacre Brahma and his followers. The day the demon arrived, three of Brahma's children were slain, including a daughter who had the power to morph. Brahma took her into his arms and upon her dying breath she transformed into a blue lotus flower. When three petals dropped to the ground Brahma knew she was gone.

"Gently he laid the flower down upon the ground and retaliated by taking the devil, Styrrgunnar's, life. Feeling that his triumph could not be celebrated because of so much bloodshed, Brahma burned a fire that night to honor those who had been sacrificed. He took his two departed boys to where he set down the lotus flower, dropped onto his knees, and wept for his losses.

"From his tears, he created the lake. Those who survived watched as the water rapidly rose, engulfing the boys, then Brahma himself, until the only thing left above its surface was the blue lotus. Many say it danced with the wind before going under to rest with her father and brothers.

"That is when Saraswati cast her spell. To protect their people from further prying eyes she created a sacred hemisphere over the village, shielding those without abilities from harm and forever ensuring it as a place of peace and tranquility. Filled with grief, Saraswati took to the mountains where it is said she became one with the earth by transforming into the river Savitri.

"The only child to survive that day was Manu. He became the forefather of my house, the ancestor who passed from generation to generation the gift of magic."

"You are a Mantrik?" I ask.

"What's a Mantrik?" Lily questions.

"A sorcerer," I answer.

"Like my father and his father before him. From Manu, Brahma and Saraswati I was chosen to continue the legacy of guarding this sacred land. To nourish those who dwell here, to welcome and guide those who find us and to convert those who choose to bathe in its holy water.

"You asked me if there are other means of transportation rather than a monumental bird or Garuda. The solution is simple. What lies below your feet will carry you there!"

Both Lily and I look to each other for answers. Her eyes widen questioningly and I shrug, unsure of this second riddle bestowed upon me today.

Quite frankly I'm starting to get a little irked because all I see below my feet are my socks, shoes and....

"Do you mean the ground?" I inquire.

Janardan explodes in a fit of laughter. I turn to Sabeena, who has a scampish smile spread across her face, then to Lily, who won't even look at me because she's too busy staring at the floor.

Jeesh! This schmo's off his rocker. All this jibber-jabber about how magical he is and the solution is what? The ground? Real friggin funny! I don't need a magician or even a rocket scientist to tell me that one. I've certainly had my fair share of being the brunt of all jokes today. I mean come on! I'm not sure

142

what this dude's playing at but I've had enough.

What lies below my feet? I'll tell you what's going to lie below it in a second!

Heatedly I stand, ready to tell this guy where to go. My foot is about to kick the pillow on which I just sat when it finally hits me. I'm not standing on the ground. I'm not standing on dirt, stone, concrete or tile. What I am standing on are piles and piles of....

"Carpet!" Lily proclaims.

Chapter Seventeen
Unparalleled

"Not just any carpet," Janardan exclaims.

Lily's eyes light up, "Really?"

Janardan nods his confirmation. Graciously he rises and strides across the pavilion to the corner behind Lily, Sabeena and me. There he bends down, grabbing the tassels on a small golden rug. With a swift tug it slides toward him, uncovering another sage and maroon mat.

He then looks to me. "Would you mind?" he asks.

I help peel layer after layer of dhurries up until we reach the one he is looking for. It is a bright purple, teal and gold carpet at least eight feet by ten. It is substantially cumbersome and together we strain under its weight, shuffling inch by inch until we reach the center of the mandapa. Janardan and I release our hold, allowing it to fall freely. With a sickening thud the rug hits the floor and a large cloud of dust rises into the air.

"Can't we use one that's less burdensome?" I choke through intermittent coughs.

"No, no. This one will do."

"But it's too large for just the two of us."

"Better to have extra space than not enough."

"And it's heavy as hell."

Janardan chuckles.

"My boy, were you planning on lugging it the whole way there?"

"No."

"Good because its job is to carry you. Not vice-versa. Nevertheless, its weight won't be an issue. I promise."

With that Janardan scuttles to the shelves, removes a ceramic mortar and brings it with him back to the table. Once there he methodically begins to grab contents out of each urn, placing them one by one into the bowl. Next, he seizes the colorful powders, taking a pinch of red, two indigo and a dash

REALM: RULER OF THE PEOPLE, GOD OF DEATH

of magenta, then crushes the contents together with a wooden pestle.

Lily and I observe intently as he works, watching as he rises, walks around the table and places a hand upon each of our heads. With a quick swirl of his fingers he plucks a hair from each of us.

"Ouch!" Lily and I whine in unison.

"You'll live," he responds then scurries back to his golden pillow. Holding the hairs in the light of the fire he inspects the root of each one, examining the rounded fleshy papilla at the end of them both.

His mouth turns up at the corners into a satisfied smile then he places the hairs into the bowl of crushed powders and holds it over the fire as he murmurs some kind of incantation.

I can't decipher the words he is muttering under his breath but it seems repetitive and during his third chant grey smoke begins to rise from within the bowl. Whimsically the smoke begins to curl and spin, changing from grey to a light green then to a bright aquamarine that matches Lily's eyes.

The smoke peaks toward the ceiling, rolls into a wave, then crashes back into the bowl, disappearing from sight. Janardan removes the dish from the fire, stands with it cradled in his left arm and begins to walk the perimeter of the rug. Around and around he strides, chanting his incantation with passionate spirit. During the ceremony he sprinkles the contents of the mortar onto the carpet with his right hand, his voice rising louder and louder, willing his effect.

To my surprise the carpet springs to life. It rises from the ground and wiggles like a worm, causing a wave to form over its surface. It then ripples from beginning to end, exiting with a loud snap that sends another large cloud of dust off into the night air.

Lily and Sabeena giggle with delight.

"Watch this," Janardan commands. He extends his fingertip to the sky, traces an imaginary line from the four corners of the pavilion, back to us then spins his finger and points to me.

Within seconds the carpet is cascading through the air following the exact route, rolling up before me then tumbling into my arms.

My eyes widen in disbelief. "It's as light as a feather!"

Janardan nods.

"Wow!" I exclaim.

"Can I try?" Lily asks, extending her arms out. Hesitantly I transfer it to her, worried that it might return to its old tonnage. But it mustn't because she's able to carry it effortlessly around the room.

"It's amazing!" she marvels.

"But fragile. The carpet is only as strong as the power bestowed upon it. Therefore, you must take extra care to protect its charm," Janardan states.

Lily nods.

"It has been created by me from the two of you. Therefore, only the three of us can command it. It is large and strong enough to haul the weight of an elephant, yet light enough for one to carry if need be. It will always be able to find its way back home, here, if you shall ever need me again and it may never, ever get wet."

"Why?" Lily asks.

"Water is pure and cleanses but it is also most destructive. It has the ability to wash away everything from a speck of dirt to the evidence of sins. It can drown people, swallow an entire village and - terminate this particular enchantment."

"Then we should get going," I interject - knowing rain is on its way and how badly I want to leave.

"You won't be able to beat the storm. You will need to stay the night."

Frustrated, I run my hands through my hair and sigh. "Will, won't – tomato, tomahto. Dude, don't get me wrong, I appreciate everything you've done for us but I need to go - so we'll take our chances."

Honestly, I was expecting more of a disagreement but Janardan simply added, "Very well then," and helped us on our way.

Not only that, he provided a pack with a tent in the event we should need one.

Within minutes we were sitting on the vibrant carpet soaring over the open plain toward my parents' home. The night sky shrouded by heavy clouds was pitch black and an eerie sensation trickled up my spine as we flew in complete blindness away from the lights of the village.

I was worried that the carpet would feel insecure and flimsy but I was wrong. Rather than sagging under our load it was rock solid. I thought the sides would buckle at the slightest shift in our weight, causing either of us to roll off easily and plummet to the ground, but instead they turned up at the edge forming a protective ledge.

Contrary to all my assumptions it also moved graciously through the air. Every turn and dive was as fluid as if I transformed into a bird and was flying myself. I tried to envision gliding alone and carefree, orchestrating every move, but I knew it was not so. I am not alone and carefree; I am with Lily and full of emotion.

The mountain range we had left just days before passed under us and in that moment a trickle of moisture ran down my cheek. Instantly I took us down to the ground, stopping in a dense patch of wood about three kilometers from where Blaze abandoned Lily and the team made the gravest mistake of our lives by not following him.

I didn't wish to be there. Never wanted to see that place again but the wetness upon my cheek was the sprinkling of rain and I had no other choice but to stop.

Lily rolled up the carpet, careful to shield it under a hearty tree branch while I pitched the tent. We clamored inside in just the nick of time. The heavens opened up with the zip of the tent's zipper and the sprinkling rain turned into a torrential down pour.

"That was close!" I remark.

"We should have stayed."

"I know - I just couldn't."

"Why?"

"Because."

"Because why?"

"Because I couldn't!" I find myself yelling back. I'm cold even though the air is sweltering. My body is overcome with feelings of longing, guilt, worry and most of all sadness because I know I haven't given myself time to properly grieve for Alia. That small cry (that I thought was so hearty) on the rooftop wasn't enough.

I was so peeved with Dmitry for listening to Kirill. How could he want to move on seconds after we found out that it was her that didn't emerge? Anger took over, engulfing me in a maddening craze so strong I had to walk it off. When we got into the village Sabeena enchanted us all with the promise of good food and rest. My vexation subsided as the need for nourishment took over.

That night I stayed awake listening to Poppy cry herself to sleep. I was so worried about how she would fare with the loss of yet another family member that it never occurred to me that I too had lost someone special.

My eyes barely closed before I was awakened again. And then I was wrapped up in this frenzy about Jaasin having gone missing, followed by worrying about what Dmitry was going to do and then the hunt to find Lily. That night at Sabeena's I couldn't think of anything other than how foreign I felt being there without my team, without my family.

When Lily came to me – reached out to me - I lost myself within her. After that I succumbed to fatigue and slept most of the day away. It was in Sabeena's front yard while I was turning her riddle over and over in my mind trying to make sense of it, that the realization of what happened to Alia started to filter in....

"I'm sorry, I didn't mean to snap at you."

"It's okay."

"No Lily, it's just that. It's not okay. Being here is not okay. I want to go home."

"So you can forget?"

Irritated, I bark, "So I can put it all behind me. And now look where we are. Of all the places we could be right now it had to start raining here, on this range, next to that god-awful cave."

"Maybe someone's trying to tell you something."

"Like what?"

"Like – don't run away."

"What am I supposed to do?"

"Remember."

I do remember. I remember the day Dmitry and I met Poppy and Alia. How weak and malnourished she was withering away on that old bed. I knew right then and there that that little girl needed help and I was going to be the one to give it to her. I transformed into her father. I'm not sure what possessed me to become Reinhart, but I figured it was important for her to realize that he lived on. Not in flesh but within her heart. Just as I need to remember that Alia will always live on in mine.

I transformed into a puppy for the first time that day. An animal I swore never to morph into and from that day forth it became my favorite because when I was that dog Alia not only smiled, she giggled! It's a sound I will never forget.

I remember how closed off Poppy became after her losses. How Alia shut down almost to the point of no return. I saw a real change in them after we moved into Dmitry's house, where over time we became a family. Turns out she just needed a bit of brightening up. I suppose that's why I want to go back so badly. Not to forget but to heal just as Poppy and Alia had done.

She came so far, especially over the past week, and now....

I have no choice but to remember.

Between my tears last night and the sweltering heat of the day my eyes feel heavy and damp as I struggle to open them. The wind is howling outside and the tent is still being pummeled with rain, which means our chances of leaving today are slim to none.

I sit up wearily to find myself alone. My body feels worn

and weak, having let so much emotion go last night. With a heavy sigh, I stand and stretch before taking to my rucksack.

Inside the pack I rummage for a canteen of water, some Moong Dal Vada and a change of clothes. After a good long chug, I bite into a tasty fritter. The outside is crispy with a soft spicy inside and I down it in two bites. While chewing I peel off my t-shirt and toss it across the tent. Looking down at the black trousers I've been wearing for a disgusting amount of time causes me to cringe.

They belong to one of the tools who tried to kill us when Poppy floated Lily and Dmitry over the Chirachnophagous-infested waters to Jaasin's cave. The thought of wearing them is revolting, though at the time I had no other choice. And since then the only other option available was a pair of Reinhart's pants, which were not only too short but a little too tight as well.

At six-foot-one, I'm a good three inches taller than Reinhart was. Jaasin, as gaunt as he is, was the only man to benefit from those clothes. Even though they were on the short side you could tell Jaasin was happy to be able to rid himself of the same pants he had been wearing for years.

That's kinda how I feel right now. Grossed out, I unbutton my slacks, allow them to fall freely to the floor, then kick them into the same corner as the crumpled-up t-shirt. It feels good to be done with them. So much so that I strut around naked as the day I was born, playing a quirky ballad of belly bongos while munching on fritters.

Luckily Sabeena's brother Salil and I are around the same build, and her mother Toya, extremely observant. Before setting off last night she thrust a pile of clothes into my hands, insisting I "Could use them."

Casually I make my way over to the bag, bend over and grab a pair of cream-colored linen trousers from the floor. I still have no underwear but that is a nasty thing to borrow - so having to go without I slide the pants up and on.

They feel incredibly comfortable. I bend and stretch,

marveling at how unrestricting they are. I punch the air a few times with my fist, throwing a few jabs and hooks before swirling around to do a roundhouse kick.

"Nnyyyeeaahhhh...hey..."

Lily is standing there staring at me. Her lips are pursed, her chin scrunched as she tries to hold in her laughter.

"Yeah, how much of that did you see?"

Taking a deep breath to steady her voice she answers, "Everything."

"Everything?" I question. My voice raises a few octaves.

Lily arches an eyebrow. I follow it up across her crinkled forehead to her hair. Dry hair!

"You're not wet."

"No."

"I thought you went out – you know, to use the bathroom or something."

"Nope." Her lips pop with the p-sound.

My eyes widen, "So?"

"I woke up early and thought I would practice using my ability until you woke up."

"And?"

"It's a lot harder to reappear, as you know. Anyway, nice song you played while slapping on your stomach. Is that something you learned in school?"

A low throaty croak escapes my lips followed by, "You saw that."

"Yeah, and the whole putting on the pants thing you had going on. That was something else."

"Glad I didn't do anything embarrassing!"

Lily chuckles.

"You know, you could have said something." I whine.

"What would be the fun in that?"

"You got me there. After all fun is my middle name."

"Really?"

"Uh, huh."

Flashing an impish smile, I casually saunter over to Lily.

Seductively I whisper in her ear," Want me to show you?"

"I think you already have," she answers.

"Not quite."

Her abdomen contracts under the touch of my hands. Quickly I pull her hips to me, her chest into mine. The fingers on my right-hand glide over a sweaty patch of skin at the small of Lily's back then up her spine and over her shoulder where I gently caress her collarbone. I can feel her pulse quicken, hear her heart begin to race as I make my way around her swollen chest.

This is more than fun, more than pleasurable. Lily and I - Earth and Realm - joined together as one. There is nowhere else I would rather be, no one else I would rather be with. Nothing else compares to this moment. Our lovemaking is unparalleled.

Chapter Eighteen
I Should Have Known

It's another rainy day, yet I haven't a care in the world. Yesterday was probably the best day of my life, spent wrapped up in Lily's arms as we bonded over the differences and similarities between our worlds. I listened to her talk about her family and told her everything there was to know about mine.

We laughed and ate, goofed off and became serious. Lily practiced disappearing and reappearing and by nightfall she was getting pretty good at it!

"Tracy?"

"Yes?"

"How is it you don't have to be naked in order to transform?" she had asked.

I laughed and told her she watched too many American movies! I have always found it funny that that is the way shapeshifters are portrayed in books and on film. You gotta love scenes when some guy strips down, transforms into a werewolf or something, then heads out on a chase. There's a huge battle, things calm down then ... boom! Suddenly he's got his clothes back on. I mean, how did that happen? Did he go all the way back and retrieve them? Because I didn't see him take the time to tether the crap to his furry leg in order for the clothing to be there afterward.

It's just preposterous. I couldn't imagine dropping my drawers every time I had to morph. What would be the point in wearing clothes in the first place?

I'm not sure whether humans believe that is how it works or if the nudity is to boost ratings. Either way it's the farthest from the truth so I took the time to explain that shifters like myself, here in Realm, always wear cotton, linen, silk or hemp. All of which come from plant life. They are natural resources. Living, breathing organisms created by our planet (just like you and I) and because of that they are able to mutate. When I wear clothing against my skin it becomes an extension of me, allowing it to then transform.

Lily was curious; she wanted to know if I would be able to make her own clothes shift with the simple touch of my finger. I had to explain that the only way I could change her clothes was if I was wearing them. The thought must have tickled her pink because she laughed for quite a while before asking for a deeper explanation.

"Lily, I couldn't touch your tank top and turn it into a leather bustier any more than I could touch you and shift you into a unicorn – because you are not me – your clothes, while on you, are not me – and transforming is my ability, which means the clothing and I would have to be connected."

"What if we were connected?"

"It doesn't work like that."

"But I'm a living, breathing organism."

"True, but a more complex organism than plant matter. People, plants and animals all have cells but it doesn't work like that for people and animals. When a fiber is removed from the plant and spun into clothing it is no longer attached to its root. When I wear it, I become its host."

"So, you could never change me?"

"I wouldn't want to. Nor could you touch me and make my clothes disappear like yours do when you vanish."

"I bet I could!"

"Ha! Not in the way I'm talking about, you couldn't!"

"I can't believe my clothes vanish. Guess I never thought of that."

"Of course they do, imagine how freaked out people would be if they didn't?"

Lily chuckled, "People back home are already freaked out by me."

"What's wrong with them? They don't know what they're missing. You know Lily, it took me a while to learn how to manipulate clothing. It's really incredible that you can do it, especially before when you didn't even know you had an ability."

154

"Really?"

"Really," I whispered into the dark, then kissed her fore-head goodnight.

Now here I am in the wee hours of the morning lying under Lily's warm body, reminiscing about yesterday as I wait for her to wake. The rain drizzles down, playing a sweet melody against the tent and I can't help but smile. I am happy - I am content – I will admit – I am in love.

For another hour I watch Sleeping Beauty until her eyes finally flutter open. Her makeup is smudged and hair is tousled as she awakens from her slumber. Our eyes lock and she smiles.

"Good morning beautiful!"

"Morning."

"Sleep well?"

She nods, "It's like a sauna in here. I'm starting to feel perpetually drowsy."

I can totally relate. For over thirty-six hours we've been zipped inside this tiny tent. The air outside was already a blistering double digit when the storm hit. A little fresh air would do us good right about now.

"Let's go out."

"In the monsoon?"

"Listen to the rain, it's nothing more than a light sprinkle now."

Lily grunts disapprovingly as she rises. Grabbing her by the hand, I pull her toward the door.

"Come on."

"Wait!"

"What."

"I want to change."

"You're going to get soaking wet and will have to change when we come back anyway."

"Exactly the point. Look at this skirt. As soon as it gets saturated I'm going to be dragging around another ten pounds or more. I need something smaller."

With that Lily prances over to her pack and pulls out a small cornflower blue frock.

"Don't look," Lily orders as she begins to unzip her raspberry skirt.

"What?"

"You heard me."

"But...."

"I know! I'm still a little too modest to have you gawk at me while I'm changing."

"I don't care what you say - I'm gawking!"

"Fine!" Lily cries, "have it your way." Then POOF! She disappears right before my eyes.

"Aw, come on!" I whine.

"Shouldn't have helped me yesterday!" she teases.

"Suppose not." I agree.

The blue dress hangs limply in mid-air, swaying to and fro, when something soft hits me in the chest. I catch it instinctively then look down to see a lavender tank top appear within my hands.

I watch the dress rise up, balloon open like a parachute, then inch down over Lily's invisible body, disappearing as it slides over her naked skin. Within seconds a reddish-pink skirt pools on the floor beneath her feet.

"That was so anti-climactic!" I groan.

Lily giggles but does not reappear.

"Lily?"

"Yes?"

"Where are you?"

"That's for me to know and for you to find out," She goads.

Giving in, I stride across the tent to where her skirt landed on the ground and grab at the air. Lily giggles from farther to my left and I take off in that direction chasing her laughter around the perimeter of the tent.

After a few laps I stop, playfully chanting, "Come out, come out, wherever you are!" The tent is eerily quiet. Slowly I tiptoe around, straining my ears for any sound. Then WHAM!

Her hands clasp tight around my eyes and she whispers in my ears, "Got ya!"

"You know, two can play at this game."

"Really?" she sings sarcastically.

"Yup." I pop the P, just as she had done to me previously.

"I'm shaking in my boots!" she prods.

"I guarantee you will be."

"Oh yeah?" Lily whispers.

"Oh yeah!" I confirm.

SNAP! I slide into a Bonnet Macaque, wrap my tail around her invisible arm, swing my furry body around, land on her back and grab hold with my hands just in time for the reaction I was hoping for.

"AAAAAAAAAAAAAAHHH!" She shrieks then takes off running and hopping about like some wild bucking bronco. In between screams she swings her hands about trying to knock me off but yelps again every time she touches me.

I take my little old world monkey hands and run them through her hair just to get her a little more riled as she circles the tent.

"AH – YAY – AH – AH!" Lily howls. Oh my god, it's so damn amusing. Cruel but so frigging funny I can't help myself. My next move is off the hook! Quickly I unfurl my tail then whip it around into her face and it just so happens to land in her mouth as she's opening it for yet another yelp.

Her reaction is priceless. Laughing my ass off I lose my grip, fall off her back and then roll to the ground where I morph back into my normal self. Howling with hysterics, I clutch my abdomen. Water floods my eyes and I can barely make out Lily who has reappeared across the tent from me.

She's on her knees, breathing hard, clutching her chest. One hand helps steady her on the ground and her eyes - (whoops!) - they are throwing daggers straight at me!

Panting, I roll up onto my knees to face her.

"Real funny!"

"I thought so," I smirk.

"Ass!"

I transform into a donkey and hee-haw before spinning back to myself. Lily chuckles.

"Mad at me?"

"No."

"Come here."

"No."

"Come on!"

"No!"

"Don't make me do it."

She smiles.

"I'll do it, I'm warning you!"

Lily stands, crosses her arms then taps her toe.

POOF! I spin back into the monkey and scream, "I told you not to make me do it!" Which I'm sure sounds to her like "O – OO – A – OO - OO - A - A - O – AA!" I then hop around playfully, chasing her as she giggles and runs away.

Standing with my back to the door I have her cornered. Lily is across from me against the back wall of the tent with her arms spread out to each side, ready to take flight at my slightest move. But instead of resuming the chase I return to my old self once again.

"I want you!" I confess.

"Do you?"

"Yes."

She tiptoes forward into the center of the tent. I follow her every move. When we're standing face to face she kisses me hard on the lips. It is quick, firm and full of passion. Pulling away she smiles then vanishes in the blink of an eye.

"Come get me!" Her voice echoes through the air. With a loud zip the door to the tent flies open and I know by the rustling of the ground cover that she has taken to the rain.

I dart after her, careful to close the tent behind me in order to protect the carpet. The sun has begun to penetrate through the remaining clouds, yet where I am the rain is still falling steadily. In a matter of minutes I am soaked from head to toe.

My linen pants are starting to weigh me down and the discomfort of them clinging to my skin is annoying. It's a no-brainer – I have to morph. Quickly I slide into a squirrel and scurry up the closest tree to get an eagle eye of the ground below.

Lily is ten feet away, fully visible and tiptoeing through the heavier brush toward the thickening trees. I charge upward to a large branch then jump limb to limb across three trees until I have closed in on her. Quietly I scamper down to the ground and over the undergrowth until I am nestled between her legs, and look up.

It takes her a good minute or two for her to realize she's not alone. When Lily first sees me it's clear she thinks I am just an ordinary squirrel. Her baby blues soften and she coos a soft "aww." So, I take my fuzzy tail and rub it against her leg. I know the light in her attic clicks on when her expression shifts. Her eyebrows furrow as she gazes suspiciously at me.

"Hmmm," she groans. "Hi there little fella. I have to say, I've never been this close to a squirrel before or had the experience of having one try to look up my skirt – TRACY!" she accuses before fading away.

I can hear branches break under her feet as she darts away. When the air grows silent a second later I know she hasn't gone too far. I then take to the trees and wait patiently for her to reveal herself.

Sure enough, moments later I find she is hiding behind the trunk of a larger tree to my right. I have to admit this game of hers is fun. But I'm not going to let her get the upper hand, so I make my way over to where she is, shift into a snake and slide down the thick trunk until I'm coiled and dangling just above her head.

Lily's pressed tight against the tree as she scans the forest for any sign of me. I can't help but chuckle. The sound escapes my mouth in a small hissing spit, instantly alarming Lily. She takes a step forward and turns around with wide eyes. I slither down, wrapping myself around a branch, then glide forward until I'm an inch away from her face. She swallows hard and takes a slow step back.

"Tracy?" she questions, "is that you?"

I decide not to respond because I'm rather curious about her reaction. Again, it's cruel but her teasing me like this is too. Then all of a sudden the thought of her running from me forms a knot in the pit of my stomach. I love a good game of cat and mouse but I find I'm suddenly tired of this chase. With this new pang of irritability, I find I've unknowingly bared my poisonous fangs.

Lily looks absolutely horrified and a wave of guilt floods over me. Without thinking I rush to hold and comfort her. My body curls around hers and I hug her tightly, as if I will never let her go.

She struggles against my loving tenderness then gasps for air. I look into her face questioningly, wondering why she isn't returning my affection. She's turning a bright shade of pink and to my horror I realize I am still the snake. I release my hold, knowing I must shift back and explain. Hopefully she will understand how stupid I've been. As I begin to do so, Lily throws me with immense force across the woods and vanishes from sight.

My body twists and morphs as I am catapulted through the air and when I land, I land hard at the base of a tree. It knocks the wind right out of me, leaving me no choice but to sit for a good five minutes in order to recuperate.

By the time I've shaken it off there is no sign of Lily. No rustling of ground cover, not a single sighting as I soar through the air looking for her. My search expands over the forest, over our camp and back toward the infamous cave.

I don't know what brings me to do it but I land on the plain outside the entrance. Changing back to myself I sit cross-legged like a schoolboy against the rock. A chill trickles down my spine, rippling through my body, causing me to shake and convulse.

It's normal, I convince myself. Especially knowing what lies within these walls, but I can't shake the thought creeping inside my head. I can't find Lily. Surely, she wouldn't dare enter again but I've got to find out. I've got to find her and there is only one way for me to do so.

My nose hits the wet ground, pulling up the mixed muted smell of the team before we entered the cave. The last time we were all together as one. It's definitely an old scent mixing with the sandy dirt and rain. I follow it to the entrance of the cave where the strongest intuition takes over, forcing me to instinctively back away from it.

This must be what Blaze felt, how he knew of the evil lurking within. If only I was the dog that day. I would have felt it too, understand as I do now. I too could have tried to stop the team from entering. But I was not the dog, as I am now, and what's done is done.

I hang my head, disappointed yet thankful not to have picked up Lily's fresh scent. I can at least relax knowing she has not come here today, which means she is still out there somewhere.

Snout to ground, I take off again, this time honing in on a musky wooded earth and grassy scent. Blaze! I follow his trail down into the woods where the fragrance envelops a large chunk of land. Clearly the place he must have camped out for the night. It's an area far enough away from the danger, yet close enough to have an unobstructed view of the mountain in order for him to keep a wary eye on Lily.

I continue on, allowing his trail to take me through the wood, up toward the entrance of the cave, then around the rock to its exit where he paces and circles about. I look up from all my tracking to think. By tracing his scent, I can deduce the fact that Blaze most likely camped out for the night in hopes that we would exit the next day. When we did not emerge he went back to the entrance only to find it sealed, just as we had done from the inside.

He then walked the mountain until he found another

mouth. An opening he still would not enter. There he paced nervously and circled about waiting and waiting for us to come out, which did not happen.

I imagine at some point that day Blaze lost hope and left. Where he went, I do not know... but his trail turns back down toward the plain. As I look in that direction I'm suddenly aware that the rain has stopped. The sun is now shining bright overhead and a rainbow dances on the horizon farther down the grassy mountain range.

The sight is spectacular! I close my eyes, trying to savor the moment, then inhale deeply. My nostrils burn and I stiffen up. *That's not right*, I think to myself, *it can't be*. I am momentarily paralyzed. The hair on my back begins to rise and I strain my eyes and ears, hoping they will help me decipher what is real or what is in my head. Either way, something doesn't smell right!

I'm about to go all Dick Tracy when I catch Lily in the distance running through the tall grass toward the forest. It's been over an hour since I last saw her and I know I've got to catch her while I can, so forgetting this rattling sensation I take off sprinting after her.

I watch as she barrels through the tundra toward the forest with extreme urgency. Concerned about the cause of her critical movement I accelerate, closing in the distance between us. I'm about two hundred yards away when I hear her cry out, "Blaze! – Wait! – Don't go! - I'm still here, Blaze! – Don't leave!"

Her words stop me dead in my tracks. I shift into my normal physique and watch bewildered as Lily stops just outside the wood. She stands there panting, out of breath.

"Blaze?" she questions.

I can't believe what I'm hearing. My mouth hangs open, shocked by her burning plea for him.

Out of the cover of the trees walks a man with the body of a horse, though it is not Blaze. This centaur is chestnut brown with long straight hair to match. He has a tight beard on his face, with heavy eyebrows.

He glares at Lily. Together they stand locked in each

other's eyes, then slowly he walks away without saying a word. Behind him trail half a dozen more centaurs, including three black stallions with skin as ebony as the night sky followed by an older gentleman. His graying hair hangs down upon his grey and white spotted hide. Behind him are two younger boys the color of soft caramel. All have long tresses and facial hair and carry bows with quivers full of arrows across their naked chests.

Lily heaves her own chest with the realization that none of the men are Blaze. Mine is hollowed, empty, stricken with grief and yet I walk to her.

Her eyes follow the centaurs as they walk toward the village where we met Sabeena. She watches intently until they disappear from sight with an abandoned look spread across her face.

"What was that?" I whisper.

She jumps, startled by my presence.

"I – I?" she stutters.

"You what, Lily? What was the meaning of that?"

"Of what?"

"Of THAT!" I point toward the wood where the centaurs arrived, then cast my hand down across the valley toward town.

"I thought I saw Blaze."

"That I got! I meant your reaction to seeing him – which you didn't by the way."

Lost for words, she closes her mouth and shakes her head.

"That was quite a spectacle – what do you have to say for yourself? What do you have to say to me?"

"Spectacle?" Her voice is harsh, protective.

"You heard me. I don't get what THAT was all about. Are you pining for him?"

"Pining?"

"Yes, pining. Are you going to repeat every stupid word I say or are you going to give me some kind of explanation?"

Lily doesn't speak.

"You owe me an explanation!" I yell.

"Fine! I miss him, all right? Are you happy now?"

"No! – Damn it – I'm not!"

"What else do you want me to say?"

"It doesn't matter what you say. I SAW how you feel about him."

Lily hangs her head to the ground.

"What have you been doing with me these past few days?"

"I don't know," she whispers.

"You don't know?" My voice rises.

She shakes her head in response.

"Jesus Christ, Lily!"

"I'm sorry Tracy," she yells, "I'm just as confused as you are!"

"Confused? – Me? You're out of your cotton-picking mind! I know that I want to be with you and no one else! I know that these last few days have been the best of my life and I know without a doubt, after that display that you don't feel the same! – So why?"

"Why what?" she snaps.

"Why have you been toying with me?"

"I'm not toying with you."

"Then what? Do you want to be with me?"

"I think so."

"You're going to have to do a lot better than that! I'm pouring my heart and soul out to you and all you can give me is a 'think so'? Do you love him?"

"Who? Blaze?"

"Yes, Blaze! Are you kidding me?"

"I don't know."

My eyes widen in frustration.

"Fine Tracy! I have feelings for him and I have feelings for you. Is it love? I don't know – I'm new to this whole thing."

"Do you want to be with him?"

"It's more complicated than that."

"Actually, it's not. What I saw is that you do. But he's a hybrid and you think you can't, so you're settling for me?"

"That's not what you saw and that's not what I'm saying

at all! Stop putting words in my mouth."

"Then what is it?"

"I don't know," she whines.

"Is that all you can say? I don't know – I don't know - I DON'T KNOW? – I DESERVE THE TRUTH FROM YOU! WHY CAN'T YOU JUST SAY IT?"

"I CAN'T TELL YOU SOMETHING THAT I'M UNSURE OF! WHEN I SAY I DON'T KNOW, THEN I DON'T KNOW!"

"THEN WHAT DO YOU KNOW?"

"I WANT TO GO HOME!"

"FINE!"

"Fine?" she questions.

"Yes, it's another one of those words you know all too well.

"YOU'RE SUCH A JERK!" Lily screams.

"ME? – You sure about that one?"

JAASIN

Chapter Nineteen
For Daviana

From the dark corridor I hear muffled voices penetrating through the thick concrete walls.

"Mackinnley?"

"Yes, Sire?"

"I think it's time you fetched our guests."

"Which guests would you be referring to? The two dozen that arrived by boat this morning – or the others?"

"Two dozen – this morning, you say?"

"Yes, Your Majesty!"

"Impressive, Mackinnley. That's four dozen this week! This may very well be the greatest of days. Have Andrick show the lot to their rooms and you may bring me the others."

"Very well, Your Majesty."

I swallow the lump in my dry throat as footsteps draw near. It's been three days with nothing more than rainwater to sustain me, yet I know my suffering hasn't even begun.

From around the corner a redheaded balding man emerges, summoning us forward. He's pear-shaped with crooked teeth, sharp nose and smiles constantly regardless of the severity of his job. He's extremely creepy and reminds me more of a court jester rather than a second in command.

I feel frozen to the spot until a squat black-haired guard jabs me in the gut, forcing me to shuffle forward. The move rattles the chains that bind me – and only me. He then leads the three of us from the hall where we had been held toward the redheaded man, who smiles even more broadly before turning and stepping through a set of oak doors.

"Ah, hem!" I hear.

"Mackinnley, must the sound of your throat clearing be so

irritating?"

"My greatest apologies."

"Very well, what is it?"

"Your guests, sire."

"Send them in."

The stocky disgruntled guard is the first to step through the threshold.

"Sir, may I present to you – Grier Dragunov..."

"Yes, I know who he is."

"Of course, you do Your Excellency!" The Merry Andrew turns to us and coaxes "Come on!"

I have no choice but to follow Kirill into the room. It is a vast charcoal rectangle with blood-red curtains. To my left is a dais that stretches from the door we entered through across the width of the room. Beyond it, on the same wall, lies a second matching doorway.

Two golden thrones sit against the wall, both upholstered in rich purple velvet. Sitting in the largest, most elaborate chair, in the center of the stage is King Theothantanos. He's wearing black leather pants, black boots and a crisp white linen shirt. Its drawstring is open, exposing most of his chest. Over the shirt is a royal blue doublet, which is casually unbuttoned. He looks every part the playboy as he sits nonchalantly waiting for us to walk in and line up in front of his perch.

Behind me the room is much longer, stretching five times its width. A red, purple and gold rug covers the pedestal, bleeds down its stairs, then runs across the center of the room. The aisle leads all the way to the end of the rectangle, stopping in front of a vast wooden double door at its end. There are no other chairs in this auditorium other than the two thrones.

The empty room feels ghostly compared to the last time I was here. The place was full of devotees and acolytes that day. An entire congregation had gathered to hear the ruling and watch the sentencing of a man who used magic while on a registered trip to Earth. Today, only the King, his second, and one guard are present, leaving me with a gut-wrenching feeling that no good can come of this.

I try to shake the thought from my mind by gazing around the room. The wall to my left is full of large arched windows allowing the sunshine to illuminate the dark chamber, while the wall to my right has two sets of smaller arched doors. Not much has changed since I was last here, but now in between those doors to my right stands a stone statue of a woman with aquamarine gems for eyes. Her face is soft and kind. It is a face I have seen before and one I will never forget as long as I shall live.

A shiver runs down my spine and I look up to Theothantanos. He's grinning at me slyly with those eerie yellow eyes and I have to pull away from his gaze before I do or say something unwise.

Mounted to the wall behind his throne is a large dragonhead plated in gold. Everything about this place, everything about him, emanates pure evil to the point where my own demonic inner being simmers to the surface within his presence.

The redheaded man continues his introduction, pointing to Kirill.

"Tracker, Kirill Borovsky and..."

"No need to continue Mackinnley – WHY is SHE here?" Theothantanos questions.

Standing next to me is a woman several years younger than me. She has long brown wavy hair with innocent chocolate brown eyes. She's small and slender and is wearing a silky white spaghetti strap dress over her tattooed skin. I find her to be extremely exposed in the dainty negligee but regardless she stands tall and strong.

Kirill ogles at her, shifting side to side either nervously or excitedly. I do not know which, but the repulsion I have for him grows stronger within the pit of my stomach. The King too gazes at her but in his eyes I see nothing more than disgust. I feel a surge of repugnance followed by great concern for her – this fragile yet sturdy stranger.

"Well, sir – she's your mistress."

"I know she's my mistress! But she's an old one – why

couldn't you fetch a younger, new one?" the King whines.

"Well, they're quite tired if you know what I mean! He, he, he..."

"You wag! Stifle your snickering whilst I have company."

"Yes, sir."

"What's done is done, escort this worn-out concubine to her seat," he huffs.

"PIG!" the woman growls at Theothantanos.

"Shut that dirty mouth of yours or I will have Grier do it for you. Do you understand – my sweet love?"

"Yes, Your Grace," the woman grudgingly replies.

"Mr. Borovsky?"

"Your Eminence."

"How is it you came to be in possession of a wanted criminal?"

Here we go.

"It started about three years ago."

"Three years?"

"Yes, Your Grace. A boy came to me looking for his father."

"Why didn't you come to me then?"

"I did not know who the man was, actually, only that he was this boy's father. There was nothing unusual at the time. Lots of orphans come to me when they are of age, so I thought nothing of it. But then one week ago the boy returned looking for another."

"Another?"

If he speaks one word about Lily, I swear I will kill him right here and now!

"Yes. During his visit I noticed the man he sought all those years ago still where I said he was. It piqued my curiosity but as long as I get paid, what do I care if the person they seek is found – or in this case, remaining lost?"

"But."

"But his actions were most peculiar and when he paid me, it was with Alexandrite!"

"Alexandrite? How would anyone get their hands on that?"

"Again, I could care less. I knew wherever he had gotten the precious gems, they were intended to not only pay me for my service but to keep my mouth shut."

"Yet here you are."

"Here I am."

"Continue."

"When the boy left he tossed my payment onto the desk right on top of the daily news. It just so happened that the main story that day was about you, Your Majesty."

"Nothing new there."

"Not for you, but for me it connected all the dots. You see it was about how you have repeatedly sentenced innocent men and women to death without so much as a trial, and yet allowed the man accused of killing the queen to live. That is when I realized this boy's father was that man!

"He hadn't moved from the spot I found him in three years prior because it was a prison! I figured the boy was trying to spring him out, so I went after him. They killed my men and took me hostage. Three days ago I slipped out in the middle of the night, but not before taking this one with me."

"What can you tell me of the others?"

"Not much other than their current whereabouts."

"It appears I am in debt for your services. Please tell me how I can repay you."

Kirill's eyes flicker to the woman in her nightie and a chuckle escapes the King's tongue. I saw how Kirill's expression changed the moment he saw her and apparently Theothantanos noticed too. There is no doubt in my mind that he wants her.

"Perhaps the lady?" the King suggests.

Kirill humbly shuffles up the stairs. Standing before the King he bows low then grunts, "Whatever be your wish, My Lord."

The King holds out his hand for Kirill to take. Kirill grasps the hand within his plump paw then kisses the ring upon Theo's finger before standing upright once again.

Despicable scum.

Slowly Kirill descends the stairs backwards until he is standing beside me once more.

"I am curious as to why you would go after the boy by yourself rather than come to me?"

"I was hoping, once I caught them, that you would be pleased enough to consider me an ally."

"I always consider those with your talent to be allies. Perhaps we can work out an arrangement, but first I am curious to know how strong your loyalties are?"

"How strong?"

"Yes."

"Easy! The boy who hired me has followed us here. He is gaining access to your castle as we speak and...."

No Dmitry, no!

"And?"

"And the other he was looking for that day – was his sibling."

"Sibling!"

That's it! My arms fly over Kirill's head and pull back, yanking my chain across his thick neck so fast. All I need is a minute – maybe two - to suffocate this animal but within seconds the two guards have me across the room and on the floor with no harm done. Kirill pants breathlessly, massaging his red neck as the King smirks.

"Jaasin my boy, is this true?" he taunts.

"I am not your boy."

"Mackinnley, alert the guards!"

Before his words dissipate off the tip of his tongue the doors on the far side of the room burst open. A swirl of air bounces around the room, then stops five feet from me.

"It's too late for that!" Dmitry declares.

"Dmitry!" I cry.

"Dad!" he croaks. I can tell he wants to come to me but the stocky guard who escorted me into this room and tore me

171

off of Kirill has one of his hands held out, palm facing up toward my son and for whatever reason this has stopped Dmitry in his tracks.

"Mackinnley, go check on the sentry and see how it is they failed to stop this intruder. You'd think I lived on a farm with the barn doors wide open for any fly to enter. Speaking of which, Meryl, you are now the property of Mr. Borovsky. You may remove your bony keester from my throne immediately!"

The redheaded man takes off down the aisle, disappearing out of the open doors through which Dmitry just entered.

"YOU HAVE NO RIGHT!" the woman shrieks.

"My sincerest apologies, son. Things have not gone as planned today. I had good intentions of entertaining you with the presence of a lavish beauty by my side. But as you can see, that is not the case, so should you take her by the hand, as you had done to my wife so many years ago, I will have no qualms about the ramifications this time."

"YOU JERK! I HATE YOU!"

"GRIER! GET HER OFF OF ME!"

The man restraining me closes his fist then takes off across the room toward the woman who is now smacking Theothantanos over and over. The King's reaction is none other than amused, which angers her more, transforming her open hands into fists. Grier picks her up from behind effortlessly and pulls her away kicking and screaming.

"I HATE YOU FOR WHAT YOU DID TO ME!"

"Not all the things I did, if I am to remember correctly!" he chortles.

"BASTARD!"

"My darling, I'm not the bastard in the room. He is!" Theothantanos replies, pointing to me.

"Leave my father alone!" Dmitry orders.

"I haven't done anything to him - yet!"

"Nor will you!"

"And I suppose you're going to stop me? All by yourself?"

"He's not alone!" a female voice interjects.

172

Kirill, Dmitry and I turn to see Winston and Warwick standing in the double doorway. The King's eyes narrow and his jaw tightens as he murmurs, "That explains the Alexandrite."

Standing next to Winston and Warwick is Naomi and Nasya, concealed within their cloak, and....

"Poppy?" the tattooed woman cries.

"Mom! – MOM!" Poppy screams, tearing after her.

The guard holding Poppy's mother drops her to the ground, swings his body forward, then thrusts his hands one after the other in Poppy's direction. Sharp daggers fly from the center of his palms through the air toward her. Dmitry sprints across the room and tackles Poppy to the ground in the nick of time.

"STOP!" the King bellows and Grier instantly ceases his assault.

A rain shower of cutlery showers down upon the floor just behind where Dmitry and Poppy land.

"Your Grace?" the guard questions.

"They are no threat to me," he assures his minion. "Allow them to continue with their reunion."

Meryl runs to her daughter, collapses on the floor, then locks Poppy in a warm embrace. As she cradles her grown baby, I now notice the young faces of Poppy and Alia tattooed onto her arms. The two kiss and cry while Dmitry gets to his feet and stands over them protectively.

"How touching," Theothantanos comments.

There's something about the tone of his voice that rings sincere and I question....

"Why?"

My voice echoes strong throughout the room. It's the first time I have truly felt confident within his presence and I won't be tricked or fooled by his momentary kindness. He has something planned for me today and this latest action is a cruel ploy for us to let our guards down. But I won't let that happen. I need to know.

"WHY ARE YOU DOING THIS?" I bellow.

He doesn't answer.

"WHY GIVE THEM A TWINKLE OF HOPE WHEN YOU KNOW YOU'RE JUST GOING TO TAKE IT AWAY? WHY MUST YOU TORTURE THEM AS YOU HAVE DONE TO ME? I WAS SIX WHEN YOU THOUGHT I KILLED MY MOTHER - AND YOU PUT ME IN THAT HOME FOR PUNISHMENT. WHY'D YOU DO THAT? YOU'VE HAD NO QUALMS ABOUT KILLING CHILDREN BEFORE!

"WHY ARE YOU TOYING WITH THEM – WITH ME? YOU SHOULD HAVE EXECUTED ME NINETEEN YEARS AGO BUT IN-STEAD YOU PUT ME IN A CAGE TO SLOWLY ROT. I'M TIRED OF YOU AND YOUR GAMES, WHY DON'T YOU JUST KILL ME NOW AND GET IT OVER WITH?"

My rant, fueled by years and years of suppressed rage to-ward this monster - no matter how juvenile it may be - feels great. The King on the other hand is livid. Enraged, Theo-thantanos jumps to his feet, "BECAUSE I CAN'T!" he roars.

The words have me lost and confused because I know he's perfectly capable. And when he steps down off the dais and gets into my face with those raging eyes I don't doubt that he would.

"I would like nothing more than to be done with you," he snarls into my face. "I despise you...." He trails off. Slowly he saunters over toward the statue of the woman with the aqua-marine eyes. Softly he caresses the stone face then whispers, "But I love her."

Since the moment I walked into the room and saw her face etched in stone, I wondered what she was doing here. Was the likeliness mere coincidence or was the replication meant as another way to torture me? But never in a million years would I have guessed Daviana's presence to be for him - because of love.

"My mother?" I question. My voice is but a whisper, "You love my mother."

"More than you will ever know. And so, you see - I am divided."

Theothantanos turns and walks back to me before con-tinuing.

"Torn between love and hate."

"I don't understand. How do you know her?"

"It was nineteen thirty-seven and I had just taken Eugenia in as my mistress. I was married to Varina at the time and you could have cut the tension in the castle with a knife. Now I like a good row just as much as I like my women, but the constant cat fighting was wearing me down and for the first time in almost two hundred years I was feeling old and worn. I needed to get away - so I gathered a crew and set off on a hunting expedition.

"Two weeks had passed and I was growing lonely as any man would. And there she was, alone in the woods. The most beautiful young lady that I had ever laid eyes on. She'd just fallen, quite hard as a matter of fact. And the power she displayed after told me we were meant to be together. I declared my love for her right there and then - before I even told her my name. It didn't matter, she knew who I was anyway.

"God, I'll never forget that day. That feeling – the way her hair was all tousled – her wild eyes. I felt a beast stir within but there was something about her that tamed me. I spent the next ten months out frolicking in the woods trying to court her. Every day she would refuse my hand. I'd never been told no before. And I wasn't angry – on the contrary, I wanted her more than anything!

"But I couldn't stay; after all I was the Ruler of the people. When I returned to the castle I learned that Eugenia had been with child and I was a father to a baby girl. I had all these women in my life and none of them were the one that I wanted. None of them was Daviana.

"Year after year I yearned for her, but she was nowhere to be found. And then out of the blue I saw her again. I'd gone into the village and there she was begging for scraps at the market. The eighteen-year-old girl I had met so long ago was now a middle-aged woman dressed in rags with a baby in her arms.

"Her suffering shattered my heart. When I demanded she return with me, I was rejected yet again. It stung, but I still couldn't force the woman I loved to be with me. I wanted her to love me of her own free will. I left, in hopes that one day she

JESSICA CANTWELL

would come to me, but not before paying several merchants in town to keep an eye on her.

"They said she would disappear into the woods for weeks on end. Where? No one really knew, but when she did venture into the village I made sure she had food, drink, supplies and a job. I could have given her anything she wanted but instead she chose the life of a peasant. Six years later she had gone and gotten herself into trouble again.

"My anger was so strong, and at the same time I had a weakness for her. I wasn't going to leave Daviana poor and alone any longer, regardless of how she felt. I swore I would do anything to be with her, even if that meant raising her bastard children. But I never had the chance...."

Theothantanos pauses to gaze up at the statue of my mother.

"When she died, I honored that promise. I took you off the street so you weren't an orphan and placed you in that workhouse so you wouldn't die. After, I went back to the castle and told my men that I had disposed of you permanently."

"I wasn't an orphan, I had a father. He was a terrible man – but still...."

Still what, Jaasin? You can't even finish the sentence. He left me there to die with my mother and he killed my wife. I realize now that he was more of a monster than the man standing before me.

"Still?" Theothantanos questions.

"I didn't kill my mother. She was struggling in childbirth and I tried to save her and my sisters."

"You mean sister."

"No, you heard me right. Sisters'"

"One baby died – but we – we lived," Naomi and Nasya state in unison. Together they lower their shroud and show themselves to the King.

"No!" Theothantanos shrieks.

I can see by the look on his face that he is repulsed by their deformity yet mystified by their uncanny resemblance to our mother. Again, the Emperor will find himself torn between the hate he has against the disfigured and the love he has for Daviana.

"NOOOOO!" he cries in anger. "It's not possible. Daviana was flawless! How could something so heinous come from such perfection?"

"My sisters are no more heinous than my mother was perfect. She had the ability to take life – and she did on many occasions, including her own!"

"I know," Theothantanos whispers. His yellow eyes are now red and glossy.

"You knew I didn't kill her all along?"

"Yes, I knew. I knew exactly what she was and I loved her for it! She should have been here by my side but instead she – she...GGGRRRRRAAAAAHHHHH!"

Theothantanos runs up the stairs, picks up the smaller throne and throws it at the dragonhead. The chair thunders against the golden armor, ricochets off the wall, then tumbles down to the ground with a heavy thud.

The King's dark hair is tousled, his clothing now disheveled, and he turns to me with an angry, unforgiving look upon his face.

"She chose you! And look what it got her!"

Theothantanos slowly saunters toward me, his chin quivering as he continues, "I set off that day with an immense crew, hell-bent on scouring every inch of that forest until we unearthed her location and rescued her from the wretched life she had created for herself.

"But I didn't get to Daviana in time. She was lying in a pool of her own blood with a dead baby by her side and you – you were holding onto her, barely clinging to life, when I found her. God gave me the strength to do right by you – the one she loved most. Then how do you repay me? You go and screw it all up!"

"How so?"

"How so? By landing yourself on these stairs – right here

before my feet! Caught for using magic in the other dimension. You put me in a bad position that day. Twenty-four years had passed without a hint of your existence. Then there you were, hauled in for something so stupid! My hands were tied. I had to punish you - the only question was how?

"We all know I am not a compassionate man. How could I avoid giving you the death penalty without everyone catching on to my ruse? I sat there pondering the options. You knelt there gazing up at me with those eyes. HER EYES! I felt like putty in your hands, weak, palpable AND I HATED YOU FOR IT! - Then Eugenia took you by the hand and it was all over. It was too late."

"I DIDN'T KILL HER!" I shout, "I didn't kill the Queen!"

The King does not reply. My eyes search for an answer within his, my ears strain for the hint of a whisper from his lips yet he remains quiet. Through the silence, I can hear my heart thundering in my chest. Hear the blood pulsing through my veins and a deep booming voice utter the very words confirming what I have suspected all along.

"He knows."

Chapter Twenty
Uninvited Guests

Engrossed by his story and hypnotized by the memory of my mother, it was as if we were the only two in the room. Now with the baritone's residual words embossed on my brain, combined with the look on Theo's face, I know the King has more unexpected company.

Turning to see who has joined us, I witness a sight like none other. Enveloping the entire entrance to the throne room is a mammoth giant, half man and half moth. He has to be around seven feet tall with brown leathery skin. Instead of hair he has soft tan patches of fuzz sprinkled over his robust chest, which matches the beige fur on his two enormous wings. His arms and legs are as muscular and thick as tree trunks, but nothing compares to his face.

His jaw is that of an insect, long and slender, yet his mouth is oddly large and extensive with small razor-sharp nubs for teeth. His nose is short, wide, and flat, with small slits for nostrils and his eyes – they remind me of a bee or an alien: large teardrop-shaped brown orbs that extend from the nose up to his forehead. He is bald except for a patch of fur that begins at his occipital bone, which runs down his neck like a small mohawk then spreads out across his back, merging into his wings.

Theothantanos observes the Moth-man then returns his attention to me, continuing as if nothing happened.

"All the years I have lived – nothing compares to that torment – whether it be physical or mental. Torture is far worse than death – "

"I didn't kill her!"

"Don't buy into this – he knows you didn't."

"– So, I placed you in that cage knowing your body would regenerate over and over and over again – "

"He placed you in that cage because HE killed the Queen and needed someone else to take the blame! Isn't that right,

Father?" the Moth-man continues as he steps into the room.

"I am not your father. You are a product of witches' brew and betrayal. My wife and brother's son!"

The King's irises are mere slits as he stares intently at his newest intruder. His face has a look of horror mixed with rage.

"Yet you didn't know that at the time of my birth, when you ordered I be destroyed, did you?"

"I had my suspicions, which were later confirmed."

"Then you killed my parents. Your own wife and brother."

"FOR COMMITTING TREASON AGAINST THEIR MON-ARCH!" Theothantanos yells.

"And yet, here I stand."

"GRIER!" the King brusquely roars. I can tell by the tone in his voice that he has commanded an unspoken order. On cue Grier turns and starts throwing daggers but before the third one escapes his palm the Moth-man has waved his mammoth arm into the air and all fire comes to a halt.

"Nice try!" the giant snickers. "You couldn't kill me the first time, what makes you think you could do it now?"

"How is this possible?"

"Ha, ha, ha, ha, ha," the Moth-man snickers, "all good things come to those who wait. But first, let's reminisce about the day of my birth and how you ordered Frida to dispose of me."

"Who the hell is Frida?"

"You mean to tell me you can't even remember her name? She was one of Queen Varina's ladies-in-waiting. A pretty little girl you enslaved to be your paramour when she was barely old enough to bleed. It was just after your daughter vanished in nineteen fifty-four – ring any bells?"

King Theothantanos purses his lips when the beast pauses for effect. Smiling in satisfaction, he continues, "Eugenia was distraught with the loss. As I heard it, she wouldn't take you back into her bed. Varina was desperate for your attention but, as always, you tired of her quickly and moved on to younger

REALM: RULER OF THE PEOPLE, GOD OF DEATH

prey. You forced her into your chambers and defiled her repeatedly.

"Before you knew it both Frida and Varina were with child, yet only one of them was actually yours, though at the time you didn't know that. When Frida's baby died shortly after birth, Varina forced her to remain on staff in order to serve as Her Majesty's wet nurse. Frida knew it was Varina's attempt to punish her for carrying your child. She hated the Queen, but most of all she loathed you!

"Then the day came for her vengeance. Varina was in labor and Frida - Frida was ready to kill the baby once it arrived. She waited patiently to execute a revenge she thought equal to the wrongs the two of you had committed against her. After twenty-three grueling hours, a baby boy was born."

"You were not a baby, you were a monster!"

The Moth-man laughs heartily.

"Of course you would think so! I am disfigured – a blemished hybrid – a...."

"MAGGOT! I should have killed you myself!" Theo-thantanos cries.

"Maybe you should have - but you didn't. Instead you ordered Frida to dispose of me. One look into my eyes and she could no longer follow your command. She hid me for a few days then was able to slip through your greasy fingers when Varina's scandal had finally broken. You were so busy with Iron Maidens, beheadings, and marrying Eugenia that you never even noticed she'd gone.

"Frida volunteered to go to the Melting Pot, secretly smuggling me onboard a vessel. She knew that that expanse of land would be a place where I could grow up surrounded by other people like me. I was ten years old when she told me the truth about who I was and what happened to me. Every day since, I have been planning my return.

"I've got to hand it to you though, it's certainly not easy to get off that continent. In nineteen sixty-six, when I was twelve, I created a loophole into the other dimension. I thought

I could use Earth as my way of travel. I had this idea that, once there, I could create another loophole, which would lead me to your door. I jumped through, not even pondering the consequences. When I was spotted, the locals had a field day, writing about me in their papers. Lucky for me, you didn't take notice.

"I realized then that whatever I did from that moment on, I had to be completely inconspicuous. I owed it to Frida to succeed. Letting me live was far better revenge than death, because as I was saying, I am a Styrrgunnarson – your brother's child – which makes me - a true heir to this throne!"

The Moth-man points his muscular arm toward the dais.

"You are nothing more than excrement discharged from the bowels of dishonorable trash....

"My name is Bera. I suggest you call me that."

"...And you will rule this throne over my dead body!"

"Precisely!" Bera snickers.

"Are you threatening me?" Theothantanos asks.

"Threatening? No. I am simply stating the truth. Call it predicting your future, if you will!"

"You don't have it in you!"

"No – not like you do. If only I had the power to take life with just the simplest touch!"

"That is some accusation!"

"My claim is the truth and you know it."

"Your theory is just speculation, conjured from within that tiny insect pellet you call a brain."

"HA! Theo, Theo, Theo – you may have been able to fool everyone for all these years, but your gig is up now. I know for a fact that you take the lives of others in order to sustain your own. Two hundred and seventy-three years old and you don't look a day over eighteen. I can't even imagine how many living creatures have perished so you wouldn't have to."

"Ah...."

"Don't interrupt – it's quite rude," Bera scolds. "As I was saying, I know all about your secret operation. How you have been luring people over from the Melting Pot under false pretenses for the last year and a half. Promising them that if they work for you, they won't have to return to the island. All they have to do is sign on the dotted line and get in the boat, not knowing that the job is to render their lives."

Bera bends down, pushing his face into the King's, then raises the ridge above his bulging eye in question. "But you uphold your part of the deal, right? After all, once they are dead there is no need to send them back. Did you know your little scam is how I came to be here today? I know for certain what their fate is. I've seen the piles of rotting corpses in your dungeon."

"Think you've figured me all out, do you? How dare you come into my home and tell such lies!"

"But he's not is he?" I question.

"Jaasin." Theothantanos pleads.

"You said it yourself earlier, I just wasn't listening. You said my mother had just fallen, quite hard as a matter of fact. And the power she displayed after told you you were meant to be together.

"I know that story - for it was one of the last ones she ever told me. My mother had been walking through the woods when she accidently fell down a steep chasm. By the time her body finally came to rest at the bottom she was near death. A doe and fawn had been grazing nearby. Instinctively she grabbed hold of the mother when it came over to smell her, taking its life and leaving the baby without care. It was an action she regretted instantly.

"You have the same ability. That is why you said you were meant to be together, that is why you fell in love with her."

"How could I not? The power she possessed – we possess – it's extraordinary. A gift from god! Imagine what we would have been able to do. United as one, there would be no stopping us!"

"Ha, ha, ha, ha." Moth-man roars. "You know what else is a gift from god?"

"What?"

"Them!"

Bera gestures to the doors where over four dozen severely disfigured, monstrous people are pushing and climbing their way into the throne room followed by an army of the King's men.

"We have had enough of your intolerance Theo. Today your reign will end. We will take back our land and slaughter your followers as you have slaughtered us!"

"And how do you propose to do so?"

"The same way you came to order Frida to dispose of me the day I was born instead of doing it yourself. The same way she decided to keep me alive and move to the Melting Pot. It is also the same way I have gathered supporters, convinced your men to ship us across an ocean, gained control over all your guards and stand here before you in this castle. I WILL RULE!" Bera bellows, "all because of the power of persuasion."

"Persuasion?"

"Want a demonstration?"

With one quick glance at me, Bera waves his hand and I instantly feel as if my body has been taken over. Robotically I am forced to walk across the room toward the King. My arms stretch out, the chains ready to wrap around his neck. I know Bera wants me to strangle him; he's persuading me to do it, yet he hasn't spoken a single word.

Kill – kill – kill – kill – the voice within chants, *all the suffering he has caused you, you know you want to do it!* My mind is clear. All these years, all my anger toward the King, yet I know this isn't what I want. This is wrong! I am screaming to myself to stop but I can't, no matter how hard I try. I am gaining on Theothantanos. His eyes, normally so vindictive, are dilated and full of fear.

"You can't kill me Jaasin! You're a healer." He quivers.

"There will be no healing with what he is about to do," Bera replies.

Oh god.

I feel sorry for Theothantanos as he begins to back away,

tiptoeing and stumbling toward the statue of my mother, yet I can't stop chasing after him. My body continues to hunt for Bera's prey. Then Theothantanos does something, which surprises and angers me all at once. He grabs Poppy's mother by the arm and pulls her in front of him like a shield.

"If you want to kill me, Jaasin, you'll have to go through her."

"So be it!" Bera roars.

My stomach lurches as I feel the command surge through my veins. *Kill her – kill them both!* It is one thing to be forced to destroy Theothantanos, who, by all means, deserves such a miserable fate, but to take an innocent life? Isn't that what this whole thing is about? Isn't that why Bera is doing this in the first place? Isn't it to reprimand the King for killing the guiltless? Or is it only the discriminated and downtrodden that he cares about?

I wish I could find my voice. I would do anything to be able to speak, to yell out all the thoughts that are in my mind right now. Luckily, Kirill does it for me.

"STOP!" he bellows.

I've never been so happy to hear that gutless swine's raspy voice before. Though I still feel that I am under Bera's control, I have stopped moving and for now that is good enough.

"Who do you think you are, yelling for me to stop?" Bera growls.

Kirill stands up straight, takes two large strides toward the beast, then gazes up into its eyes most confidently. Without saying another word, he spins on the spot. A small funnel cloud engulfs his obese body and in a split-second Kirill vanishes, leaving Alia standing in his place.

Poppy, Naomi, Nasya and Dmitry gasp. I feel the corner of my mouth turn up into a smile and know Bera is losing his grip.

"Bera, my name is Alia Kruger-Meyer."

"Alia?" Meryl whispers.

Alia turns to look at her mother, smiles, then returns her gaze to Bera.

"The woman you have sentenced to death alongside the King is my mother. I will not let you harm her."

"And I will not let you order me around," Bera growls back. "Buzz off you pesky little fly!"

"I could say the same to you!"

"You little...." Bera charges Alia, yet she doesn't flinch. He stops just short of contact and stands over her a good two and half feet in height, heaving his massive chest in her face.

"Let my mother go and I will kill Theothantanos for you. No persuasion required."

Bera bends down curiously. "You?"

"You heard me!"

Again, Bera chuckles heartily.

"Revenge is a dish best served cold. I have been planning this for quite some time." Alia states.

"Have you now?"

"Indeed!"

"Why?"

"Because he took my mother from me when I was three, killed my father, and now he's after my friend. Someone has to stop him."

"And you think that someone is you?"

"Why not?"

"You're nothing more than a small girl with big dreams. What could you possibly do to him?"

"GGRRRRRAAAAHHHH!" Alia screams. She turns and thrusts her hand toward the King. Instantly he begins to wail in agony, then lets go of Meryl. Alia disappears in a flash, sprints across the room and returns half a second later with her mother in her arms. With a satisfied look she gazes up at the beast.

"You are quick, I will give you that."

"As well as my mother's freedom."

"Take it! She is not my target."

"Theothantanos," Alia confirms, "I have the ability and the desire...."

"But you are a child. And I will not let a child do my bidding for me."

Bera snaps his fingers, and when he does a single dagger flies from Grier's hand through the air toward the King. The next thing I see is Theothantanos with his fist wrapped around the knife, holding it about an inch from his chest. At first I thought he caught it in mid-air, then I notice the crimson spot on his shirt.

I watch as the stain grows from the size of a pea to a silver dollar, bleeding out across his chest, then I hear the thud of the knife hitting the floor. I see the King's eyes widen in terror then feel his icy cold hand grab mine. He squeezes my fist tightly as his dry lips mouth the word *Help!*

Could it be that he wants me to heal him? After all that he has done to me?

But before I can decide, give an answer or even register the blurry chain of events that have catapulted me into his hands, I sense the life inside myself being drained from within.

I begin to feel lightheaded and dizzy. My eyes are starting to lose focus and my head throbs with a dull ache. There is a high-pitched buzz ringing in my ears. A combination of cheers from Bera's vengeful crowd mixes with the shrieks of horror from my family.

I hear Dmitry cry out, see his hazy silhouette struggling to break free from Winston and Warwick's hold, knowing they won't let him touch either of us to help, and the small part of me that is still lucid is grateful for that. Theothantanos could easily take any of their lives - much faster than mine.

I could heal the King with my ability if he let me, but instead he is using his against me. The result is a long-drawn-out battle of life versus death. My knees buckle and I fall to the ground, pulling the King with me.

I look up to see his face contort as it begins to age and wrinkle. His hair is slowly thinning and losing pigmentation. He's kneeling over me with bloodthirsty eyes, bound and determined to do anything necessary to stay alive, even if that means taking Daviana's son.

He squeezes my hand hard and I feel a surge pulse through my veins, pulling me into the darkness. My body begins to seize as it tries to regenerate itself. He clutches my hand again and I feel myself convulse once more.

I am slipping away. It is only a matter of time now. I gaze to Dmitry as my eyes begin to glaze over then to Winston, Warwick, Naomi, Nasya, Poppy and Meryl. *How nice that they have found each other*, I think to myself before looking at Alia. Small little Alia, who duped us all.

She certainly is a firecracker! She is putting up a grand fight as Bera holds onto her small frame. She's yelling at him, "Let go of me!"

"Leave it alone."

"No, he's killing him!"

"And he will kill you too."

"What do you care?"

"About your life? Nothing."

"Then let me go!"

"He will take your soul in order to survive. I want him dead!"

"Then I will kill him!" Alia rages. With that she slaps the tiny palm of her hand against Bera's bare stomach, causing him to yell in pain as if he had just been burned with a hot branding stick. His grasp on her releases and she slips through his fingertips, turns, and runs toward me just as a bright white light enters the room, illuminating the shadows and scattering Bera's spectators like a bunch of roaches.

"No need!" a voice rings from within the light. A bright white Centaur emerges from the gleam with his bow loaded. He takes two more steps into the room then releases his arrow. A spark ignites its tip, transforming the white arrow into a bolt of lightning which flashes across the room.

"Muraco!" Theothantanos mutters then lets go of my hands.

LILY

Chapter Twenty-One
Confusion and Anger

Jerk, Jerk, JERK!

Grrrr! If only I had a slice of pizza, some Fritos and a soda to wash down all this aggravation. I have enough anger to eat through a Kraft Foods factory yet not enough energy to actually continue or even end this argument with Tracy. So, for once I actually shut my mouth and begin to brood in silence.

I thought I saw Blaze. So what?

'Pining.'

I mean exactly what is Tracy getting at with that? Yes, I miss and long for the return of my friend. Blaze was the first person I met here in Realm. Might I remind Tracy that it was after I was attacked, forced through a portal, and deserted by both him and Dmitry!

Blaze took me in, befriended me, and protected me. Of course I have feelings for him. Is it love? How am I supposed to know? I've been through days of warfare and treachery with little to no sleep, which has only amplified the bazillion feelings I have bouncing around this crazy head of mine and none of them seem to be easily identifiable. I'm as confused as ever.

Honestly, I haven't had a boy look my way ... like ever! Now I have two men I am attracted to. Blaze with his golden-brown skin, muscular physique and red wavy hair. I love his mannerisms and the way he talks; so mature and knowledgeable. His strong face is beautiful, with his square chin and thick eyebrows. I love seeing his dimples emerge every time he smiles. It's more than attractive and I will admit, here to myself, that yes, I have yearned to kiss his thin rosy lips on more than one occasion.

No matter how ticked off I am at Tracy, he is right about

my feelings for Blaze. He's also right in assessing the fact that I know he is a hybrid and therefore we cannot be together. But he is wrong to assume that I am settling for him or toying with his emotions.

Tracy acts more my age even though he's three years older. He's hip, completely urban, and has a small part of the devil in him that I can't resist. His body is flawless, his face is inviting and I am undeniably addicted to his charms. Furthermore, he is open about wanting me, which makes him my drug of choice.

Blaze left me at the cave. It took a while for me to digest the rejection I felt. When he came with me on this expedition a part of me thought we would be together indefinitely. I was safe in his arms and relied on his presence, on his intuition. Yet, I didn't follow it. I chose my family instead.

I chose a path that he would not – could not take. I made the decision. Was it the right one? I'm not sure I will ever know. There are moments when I believe it was the right thing to do, and then there are times like this. What I do know is that there is no going back. After we exited the other side of the cave I realized that what I had lost pales in comparison to losing Alia.

Blaze was out there somewhere, alive and well. One day, if I am really lucky, I might even get to see him again. Tracy lost something that day he will never get back. He was distraught. He needed me just as much as I needed him, so I made another decision. I took his hand and followed him away from the madness. Tracy's path was supposed to be our way out; instead it lead to another crossroad.

A lot of things were going through my mind during that walk. I wondered what it would be like to live in Realm without having a father that was accused of killing the Queen. What it would be like if we didn't have to run and hide or battle hideous beasts. What would everyday life be like here if things were normal?

Normal? Normal?

I churned the word over and over in my mind. What does

that word even mean? I heard Blaze's voice in my head whispering, *"Normal means conforming to a standard; usual, typical or expected."* I smiled to myself as I pondered the definition. As far as I could see there was no normal in Realm. Everything and everyone here is unusual, atypical and unexpected.

I started to think about life back home on Earth in Baltimore. How there is no conforming to a standard there as well. We don't all wake up at the same time, do the same job and wear the same clothes. We are all from different ethnicities; eat different food, pray to different gods, and have separate political views....

There is no usual, typical or expected. We are all different, and that - I suppose - is what normal is. I wondered why was it so hard for my peers to accept me with my white skin and hair, or my family with their eccentricities? After all, Annie has bright orange hair with freckles, Rachel is Jewish, Sean is a bookworm who could be regarded as a nerd and Spencer is a jock.

I realize that by cataloging them into specific groups I could be viewed as the judgmental one but the simple truth is that most people are pigeonholed in some way or form. My thoughts on Annie, Rachel, Sean and Spencer are mere fact. I'd never persecute, harass or be hostile to someone because of their individuality like others have done to me.

I toyed with the fact that maybe it was me who was being cynical, then decided, for the most part, that I am more of a realist. We are all different and yet I was the one being bullied back home in Baltimore. It is a topic I continually return to no matter how much I want to forget. Their actions cut deep, scarring me forever, and consequently I will always be haunted by that time in my life.

Since the moment I fell from the sky and hit the ground here in Realm I have been accepted for who I am and what I look like. There is only one here who looks down upon the natives. One who exiles those who are not born of a certain caliber. My mind wandered back to Blaze. I thought about how unique and how breathtaking he truly is and how I wouldn't change him for the world.

The King and all of his perceived opinions sickens me. What he has done to my father, what he would do to my aunts and what he will do to us if we are caught is unsettling.

My skin prickled with the thought, then Tracy squeezed my fist within his as if he knew something was wrong.

"Whatchya thinking about?" he asked.

I looked up into his light green eyes and smiled.

"Nothing."

He grinned a sad little smile and nodded. My heart sank and my stomach lurched in that moment. Tracy threw in the towel and I let go of my father's hold in order to follow. How easy it will be for the two of us to end this. Walk away from the manhunt, free. The only problem is that it wasn't over for my father and Dmitry – not by a long shot.

I chose a path that they could not take. I chose a man over my family that time and neither decision, to leave Blaze or to go with Tracy, felt right. My heart began to accelerate as anxiety took over.

We had just entered a beautiful town bustling with dark-skinned, dark-haired people and all I could think about was that this was the end for me. I left without saying goodbye and as a result I felt uneasy. That's when Dmitry's voice cut through the air and settled my heart.

He was calling for Tracy who was still angry and exasperated. So naturally Tracy waved him off. Then Dmitry cried for me. I could sense the desperation in his voice. I wondered what was wrong. I thought about so much during that walk, yet it never dawned on me to question why Dmitry and the others followed. I turned just in time to watch my brother collapse.

Sabeena must have been an angel sent down from above to rescue us. We were starved and dehydrated, tired and dirty. Out of the kindness of her heart she gave us food, shelter and allowed us to shower, which in turn gave us a fresh outlook on our quest. We all felt rejuvenated within her presence. And with a new plan of escape set for the morning, one where we could all walk away free, I fell into a deep slumber.

The morning brought chaos yet again. I wasn't sure what all the commotion was about. It seemed everyone but me was fully aware of what was going on. I woke to Dmitry slamming doors, kicking pillows and cursing Kirill.

I quickly deduced in my grogginess that my father was missing and Kirill was the culprit. Emotions were running strong. Dmitry even spat at Sabeena before apologizing and calling the whole thing off. He said the mission was over and ordered us all to go home.

I just met my brother a few days ago and he already has a bad habit of getting under my skin. I am so tired of him barking orders at me! He should be asking for my help rather than sending me home. He acts like a male chauvinist pig commissioning me to the kitchen just because I have female genitalia rather than having me join in the attempt to rescue our father.

I've gotten into it with Dmitry a few times since he pulled me here and this time was no different. I was pissed! He couldn't have rescued Jaasin in the first place without my help; therefore, I felt I had every right to go. Only I didn't even get the chance to argue my point before he got physical with me. When Dmitry grabbed my wrist I lost it, kicked him in the gut and took off!

I flew down three flights of stairs, out into the courtyard and back into the market where I bumped into and collided with a few innocent bystanders as I made my way out of town. My mind was racing. I figured *screw Dmitry; I'll rescue Jaasin myself*!

I ran all the way to the outskirts of the village to the spot where Dmitry collapsed. I stood there staring at the ground where he had lain, then to the mountains beyond, the rocks where Blaze walked away from me and where we lost Alia.

I suddenly realized I had no idea where to go. I didn't even know where I was. I was no longer full of piss and vinegar. In addition to being angry I started to feel scared, lonely and depressed.

I doubled back into the village, circling through the buildings as I walked. It reminded me of when I used to recklessly meander through Baltimore thinking about getting picked off. *How stupid*, I thought to myself. And what's even more disturbing was that this idiotic behavior of mine took place just one week ago.

I knew the right thing to do would be to go back with my tail between my legs and apologize to my brother for socking him, but in truth I hadn't calmed down enough to return. I knew if I did Dmitry would still be insistent upon my returning home and I wasn't ready for that either. I miss Orvah and Mac something terrible but I've grown so much over the last week.

Rather than going back to my boring life of solitude and dead-end job, where I read fantasy novels to escape my jejune existence, I needed to continue. Push forward through all the un-pleasantries; explore the cause of my development and see things through. How could I possibly close the book now before the story ends?

For the first time in my life I felt like I could breathe. I was gaining a new sense of appreciation for myself and was growing excited about the woman I wanted to be. Something was bringing me out of my shell, allowing me to blossom, and I felt liberated. I owe it all to Realm. Or at least I think so, which is why I didn't go back to Dmitry and the gang.

Instead I walked down to the water's edge to clear my head and reflect upon all the feelings I had. Dmitry had to understand why I wasn't ready to go home and why I needed to be a part of his escapade till the very end.

In order for me to get the point across I had to sort through what was going on inside of me. I stood there staring at the water, my mind drowning in thought. Then I closed my eyes, took a deep breath and turned my head down toward my feet. I opened my eyes, wiggled my toes and watched as my feet carried me down the stone steps toward the water, counting to myself as I went.

It is a silly quirk of mine. Counting each stair as I walk up or down them. But the idiosyncrasy did its trick and by the time I reached the landing I felt calmer. I drew in a deep breath and lifted my gaze upward in time to see a man standing before me, a human barrier blocking my passage to the water's edge. He had not been there when I arrived, nor had I heard him present himself in the short amount of time that my eyes were closed. I had not felt his presence or seen his shadow while I watched my footsteps and counted the stairs. It was as if he materialized out of thin air.

The one thing I have learned about my ability is that my emotions get the best of me, making it easy to vanish. However, reappearing has proven more difficult. So, I knew I was still unseen while standing on the ghats. What I didn't know was who this man was or if he was aware of my presence. I waited for a long moment, gazing directly into his rich chocolate eyes, waiting for any sign of recognition. He showed no emotion; he stared right through me and never spoke a word. I lowered myself onto a step and sat there watching him in silence.

A few minutes later Sabeena appeared. Quietly she tiptoed down the stone treads and bowed to the man before us. He returned her salutation with the nod of his head and a low bow. His fingers reached up to touch his forehead and when his body returned to its upright position he whispered "Salaam."

His eyes locked onto Sabeena's for several moments. She nodded as if responding to an unspoken command then took a seat on the same step as me, not more than a foot from me. She sat there in silence for over five minutes, so when she spoke I was taken by surprise. Even more so, by the single word she uttered.

"Lily."

"How did you know I was here?"

"By the presence of my friend here," Sabeena replied, motioning toward the man.

I didn't know what to say to her; yet there were so many questions bouncing around inside my head.

"Why did you come here?" Sabeena questioned.

"It's a long story."

"I meant to the lake."

"Oh."

"To cleanse yourself?"

"I suppose."

"Drinking water releases toxins from your body. Washing with it sanitizes your skin. So, it's natural to think bathing in it will wash away your worries, cleanse the soul, though that is not always the case. Some quandaries run much deeper. Pollution within your heart and mind, only you can rid yourself of that. This lake will not wash away your pain."

A tear bubbled to my eye and I was grateful Sabeena couldn't see me wipe it away. She was right and I felt ashamed about how transparent I really was. Could everyone see right through me, just as she had done?

I was mortified that a girl my own age had the power to make me feel like a child. I knew more than ever that it was time for me to grow up.

"You're right, Sabeena. I have a lot of sorting out to do."

"Don't we all?"

In those words, I took comfort.

"You do?"

"Of course."

"But you seem so put together."

"I think I am. But when you get down to it, I'm still a teenager. There is still a lot for me to learn. There are experiences to be had, and mistakes to be made. Sorting out, as you put it, and handling the way we sort it are two different things."

"I see."

"In a way."

"What's that supposed to mean?"

"No need to get defensive. What I mean is that you are like a newborn. What you see is so vibrant and exciting, but you don't understand the complexities."

"Of what?"

"Of things like this lake. You see nothing more than a refreshing pool on a hot day. A place to soak, splash and sink your troubles."

"Not true!"

"No?"

Sabeena raised a thick eyebrow in question, gazing in my direction with her piercing eyes and perfectly symmetrical face. She pursed her thin lips and raised her square chin. I was angry with her for calling me out like she did, jealous of her beauty, but at the same time admired her brutal honesty. Everything boiled down to the fact that I wanted to be just like her.

"You're right," I confessed.

"I know."

"You don't have to rub it in."

"That is what friends do," Sabeena replied. In one fell swoop she reached out and took me by the hand.

"My Lily, there is so much for you to learn here in Realm, for example the power of this lake. It is so profound. Haven't you wondered why no one has taken to it in this blazing heat?"

Her adjective of choice made my heart skip a beat. And then I realized how true her statement was. There's nothing better than a cool dip on a hot day. Kids back in Baltimore would be running through hydrants or pleading with their parents to take them to the sandy beach at Gunpowder State Park. For a moment I paused to think about how odd it was that I hadn't questioned the lack of bathers myself, then quickly concluded that it was most likely due to Baltimore Harbor. Back home we are also surrounded by water that no one occupies, because it is not safe for swimming.

"No, not really," I admitted.

"Baby eyes!" Sabeena taunted.

"Why isn't it safe?" I question.

"You will never find a more guarded body of water."

"I don't understand."

Sabeena smiled gently. "This lake was formed many centuries ago in the aftermath of great tragedy. Its creator lies at its bottom alongside his beloved children where they shall remain together for all eternity. Some say it was his dying wish to be able to provide unity for those whose hearts beat as one. That is why this lake is an enchanted body of water capable of transformation."

"What exactly does that mean?"

"We live in a world with many species. Those who may be of the same class are often born different. And those differences have been ostracized for many generations. Mixing breeds is not only frowned upon here in Realm, it is now classified as a crime. But it is our heart that chooses for us. Who are we to deny it the love and passion for which it beats? All for the sake of one man's rule? It seems so silly.

"Say you do everything right, follow the Kings law and still bear a child with a deformity. The baby would be dubbed a monster and sent to the Melting Pot before the cord to the placenta was cut - before it could suckle your swollen breast. And what if you fell in love with a man who had no talent at all? That's to say if there are any left on this land for you to find that haven't been enslaved. What would you do then? Dismiss your soulmate, sequester yourselves, or live in exile?"

Sabeena paused. I wasn't sure if it was for dramatic effect or if she really wanted me to answer the question. All of her possible conclusions stunk, quite frankly.

"I don't really like any of those options."

"Neither do I. I believe you should always follow your heart. If it is meant to be – it is meant to be."

"How so, after all you spoke about the King? What hope do people have?"

"The Lake!"

"You said it unites, what exactly does that mean?"

"It means, when one has a powerful affinity for another and they bathe in this water they will morph, taking on true love's form. Those without power immerse themselves within the pool with their second half - this allows them to absorb the other's ability. Do you understand?"

"Yeah – so theoretically if I fell head over heels in love with a turtle and it loved me back, I could become a slow-moving reptile just by swimming in this lake?"

"Funny how you chose to be the one to transform into an animal with a shell to which you could retract your head and hide."

"Don't read too far into it! It was only an analogy."

"So, you want to become a turtle?"

"No! Gosh no!"

"So why not have this reptile transform into a handsome man instead of the latter?"

"I suppose it's easier than kissing a frog."

"Now you want to kiss frogs?"

"No!"

"You are a weird, silly little girl!"

"It's from 'The Frog Prince', an old fable from my childhood. Long story short, when the girl kisses the frog he turns into a prince. Haven't you heard of it?"

"All too well, my sweet Lily!"

"So, you were teasing me?"

"Guilty as charged."

"I'll get you back one day, you know. Once I've gotten to know you better."

"I'm sure you will."

Sabeena squeezed my hand and sighed, "We were meant to find each other."

"Maybe we should go for a swim!"

Sabeena roared with laughter, "The time is not right. That is why my friend is here. I told you, you would never find a more guarded body of water."

"He knew I was here all along?"

"Yes, he felt your presence. As I'm sure he still does."

"I found out I had this power a few days ago, and I don't know how to control it."

"Meditation might help you reappear. Why don't you

give it a try?"

If Sabeena was frustrated she never let on. I swear we sat there for three hours while I tried to gain clarity. Sabeena insists that it was only for a good twenty minutes, after which she realized it was a lost cause (not exactly her words) and thought it best we return to the others. After all, they were ready to leave before she departed to look for me.

As soon as we stood and walked up the flight of stairs, the mysterious man followed. Sabeena and he walked stride for stride together toward the temple steps, at which point they bowed to each other and parted ways.

Sabeena and I made our way back to her guesthouse and the rooftop garden where I stormed out on the others only to find out that they left without me. I yelled and screamed a few choice words, more pissed than ever. After all we'd been through those last couple of days I meant nothing to them. They used me and threw me to the gutter, like trash.

Sabeena apologized, saying she never would have packed up the rucksacks full of supplies if she knew they were going to do that to me. I was welcome to accompany her back to her farm and stay as long as I wanted. F-it, I thought. What else was I going to do?

Chapter Twenty-Two
Limbo

Sabeena's friendship comforted me and our walk through the golden prairie in the bright sunlight eased my nerves. Chahna, one of Sabeena's camels, sensed my presence and took it upon herself to nudge into me over and over until I took her by the reins. She began to nuzzle her soft snout into the back of my hair then nibbled and pecked at me most curiously. I giggled and scratched her chin and when I did so, Chahna cuddled up to me in return, which warmed my spirits.

I was visible once more strolling next to Chahna no more than a mile out of town when I heard him call my name. And sure enough, there he was standing in the tall honey grass, cloaked by the glow of the afternoon sun.

Tracy, with his soft blonde hair swept over his right eyebrow and the other arched in question. His mouth turned up into a rascally grin. He was wearing a heather grey t-shirt that used to belong to Poppy's father, which was too small and hugged every one of his muscles in all the right ways. He still had on the black trousers that hung low around his waist and the sight of him standing there made my heart accelerate.

My voice cracked as I called out to him. And when he ran to me I was drawn to him. Pulled together like two magnets, his positive charge to my negative, and we clicked together in an electrifying embrace.

"I told you Lily, no matter what happens, I'll protect you," He whispered and with his promise came a flood of remembrances, words and actions of his that rang true since the moment I met him.

Tracy came back for me today just as he had done when I fell from Dmitry and landed in the Melting Pot.

He locked me in his arms when Tearlach and Vilhelm came for us after we had freed my father. He sheltered me from harm and kept me quiet so that the king's guards wouldn't learn of my presence.

"*I'll never let you go, Lily, I'll never let you go,*" he assured when they attacked. Our bubble was being teleported and at the time we didn't know where we were going to end up. Luckily our destination was Alia and Poppy's farm.

Tracy had been the one who pulled me from the Caricorpion's lair after my father let go of my hand. He held me tight and stroked my hair while cooing, "*It's alright, it's alright.*"

I'll never forget his compassion after witnessing Scylla and Charibdys's massacre, even though I hadn't welcomed it at the time. There had been so many times along the way when Tracy was there for me both physically and emotionally.

Later that night after I snuck into Tracy's room and tucked into his arms I thought about how he dove into the freezing water to save Dmitry and me from the Chirachnophagous.

I laid there with my cheek pressed up against his warm skin listening to the beat of his heart, knowing that he nearly died transforming into that beast. Remembering how his own life's worth didn't matter to him the second he saw my face. Tracy was more concerned about my safety and thanked the lord that I was all right.

"*I don't know what I would do without you,*" He murmured, then pulled me into his naked body and kissed me ever so passionately.

I hungered for more with the recollection. Ever so softly I kissed his chest. Tasting the salt on his warm flesh made me realize how ravenous I had grown. That night and the days to follow I voraciously devoured every exhaustive moment we shared.

And though this was new to me, every time we were together I felt something was lacking. Yet I returned to his embrace again and again hoping he would eventually fill what was missing.

My mother once told me that not all problems could be solved with food. She was right about how I used it to fill a void. (And would still be using it today if it was easily accessible.) I suppose I was doing the same thing with copulation.

So, in a way, I am not being truthful to Tracy. Which makes me the jerk and is the reason why I shut my mouth. Seeing the hurt in his eyes and the anger in his movement as he packs up our camp only makes me want to reach out to him. But what good would that do for either one of us?

Not a word is spoken as he stows the tent and loads the carpet, nor as we ride through the crisp air. I watch the afternoon sun fall, changing the heavens from a clear ice blue to wild magenta, purple and orange. Tracy seems to soften with the colors of the sky, finally making eye contact as the stars begin to show.

I smile and sigh an unspoken apology. He returns the gesture with a flirtatious grin and sparkling eyes. Neither one of us utter a word, allowing the silence to clear the atmosphere between us.

The sky darkens as we descend upon a thick forest. Our carpet navigates fluidly through the trees, twisting and turning until we slow to a halt in front of a darling little cottage nestled between two large oaks. Its white paint is crackled and peeling, the deck settled and un-level underneath its covered porch. All the windows are closed with the curtains drawn.

Tracy looks relieved as he holds out a hand for me to take. I follow him up the rickety steps then wait as he pulls the screen door forward and turns the knob of the heavy wood door behind it. It squeaks open, revealing a room darker than the night outside.

Swiftly Tracy strides in. Cautiously I tiptoe behind. Unable to see my hands in front of my face, I wave my arms around searching for anything that I might stumble or bump into. I hear the floorboards whine underfoot as Tracy glides around in the pitch-black room followed by a tiny click.

A light pops on, illuminating the house, and I freeze. Tracy's standing to my right next to a floor lamp that is in the corner of a small gathering room between two gold Bergere chairs. He steps out, scooches around a white settee and past a distressed coffee table with iron legs and takes me by the hand.

"It's okay," he assures.

I realize I'm partially crouched, as if I were a cat burglar prowling for goods when the light came on and caught me.

"I must look ridiculous," I note as I stand upright.

"Ridiculous? No, just scared."

"I'm not." I balk.

"Didn't say you were – just said you look it."

Tracy's tone is sharp and he lets go of my hand.

"I'll be right back," he mutters then disappears down the dark hallway to the right of the gathering room.

I feel silly and exposed as I stand a foot and a half inside the door. Looking around, to the left of me is a wood table surrounded by eight chairs, behind it rests a quaint little kitchen. I walk around marveling at the rooms, how simple and content they are with just the things needed to live. The saying *less is more* comes to mind and I can't help but agree. Seeing a place so free of clutter is refreshing.

My finger is rolling over the empty counter top, caressing the soft old wood when Tracy emerges. He's changed into a fitted pair of jeans, a black t-shirt, and canvas shoes and is wearing a look of concern over his face.

"Something wrong?"

"No one's here. I thought they'd be back by now."

"Your dad?"

"What? – No! - Lily, what are you talking about?"

"I don't know. I thought you wanted me to meet your parents."

"I want nothing more than for you to meet my family – but I need YOU to want to meet them. When you do, then I'll take you there. Just a few hours ago you said you wanted to go home – remember? And by the tone in your voice I know it came from the heart. So that is where I'm taking you."

A few hours ago I was being accosted by Tracy, demanding that I define my feelings for him and Blaze. He had me pinned with my back against a wall and I knew the conversation had to end before I blurted something out that I didn't mean or couldn't take back. I had to discuss my fondness for both men with someone other than him. I needed a friend like Sabeena to help me sort through it.

Then this flash of anger surged through me because more than anything I wanted my mother. I've wanted her, needed her, for so long. I was so damn mad that she wasn't there to help me, to add the two cents she so often paid me when I visited her. In all my frustration I yelled – screamed as a matter of fact - that I wanted to go home.

"I was angry."

"So was I."

"I don't want to go."

"Nor do I want you to."

I smiled, relieved that we agreed on something today. Then Tracy added, "The funny thing about anger, Lily, is that it often gives us the courage to say the things we normally wouldn't admit."

And he was right about that too. I'm just as torn between wanting to go home and wanting to stay. Again, I decide it's best to change the subject.

"Where are we then?"

Tracy smiles, "This is your father's house. Naomi, Nasya raised Dmitry here. I moved in a few years before Poppy and Alia. Now Winston and Warwick live here too. It's our home."

"It's beautiful."

"You're beautiful."

"Tracy."

His smile fades and his eyes lower. "I think we should go now."

And for the first time, I agree.

Three hundred and six stairs later we've reached a dirt hole in the ground large enough to hold a circular table, four chairs and little else. Tracy's lantern is enough to illuminate the entire space, allowing me to take it all in, which really isn't much. I can see ledges have been carved into the earth to make homes for several candles and on the center wall stands a heavy oak door. That's it! – nothing more.

A sickeningly sweet vanilla scent mixes with damp decaying earth. The result is an aroma so vile and pungent it makes me dizzy. Combining that with the physical exertion it took me to descend three hundred and six stairs and before you know it....

Yup - I passed out!

I'm not sure how long I was out but when I came to I could see that all the candles had been lit. This in turn caused the vanilla scent to intensify, which makes me retch. Now a new stench is wafting through the air and I seriously begin to think that this catacomb will be the death of me.

I'm a hot mess and yet Tracy is here by my side, pulling me up off the ground and setting me down onto a chair.

"Lily, are you alright? What's going on?"

"The smell - these candles – I can't breathe - it's killing me."

"I dropped the light when you fainted. I caught you before you hit the ground, but the lantern – it broke - I'm sorry. Without the candles, we won't be able to see."

"I understand," I croak then gag before adding, "I need to get out of here."

"You need your strength. As soon as I open that door and we make the jump you need all your wits about you. One wrong move and we both end up in the grey – and believe me Lily, we don't want that to happen."

"I'm ready."

"I don't think you are."

"Tracy, I'm ready!" I growl through clenched teeth while suppressing the urge to purge.

"I sure as hell hope so."

The door opens and a cool crisp gush of air rushes through me. Tracy grabs a hold of my waist and yells, "Hold on to me and don't let go!" Complacently I put my arms around his shoulders, linking my fingers together at the nape of his neck, and press against his body. Tracy's torso clings to mine. His muscles tighten as he shifts toward the rushing air and the room begins to spin. Seconds later we are surrounded by complete blackness. Once more I feel that rush of cold air followed by immense heat and pressure.

Seconds later we barrel through another door, landing in a heap on a dusty unkempt floor. Tracy scrambles to his feet, scoops me up before I can even open my eyes and twirls me behind his back. In one fell swoop he closes the door and presses me tightly against it. Breathing hot breath into my ear he whispers most urgently, "Last time I was here things didn't go as planned, especially with Damien. He might not be too happy to see me, so if things don't go well I want you to run. Get out of the bar and go home. Don't worry about me, got it?"

Nervously I nod.

Immediately Tracy twirls around. I can see through the space under his arm that we are at the very end of a dark hallway. There are no other doors or windows and blocking the exit is a massive shadow, just as tall and wide as the hallway itself.

My scalp tingles and the hair on the back of my neck rises. I have this gut feeling, a sense of déjà vu calling to me.

Tracy walks slowly toward the figure. I follow, periodically peeking around Tracy to see what's going on. With each step, we grow closer and closer to the colossal man until I can just make out that he is bald and standing with his back toward us. Still Tracy creeps closer, tiptoeing as if he were walking on eggshells.

"Damien?" Tracy questions.

"Shhhhh," the man responds, then extends his arm, blocking the passage entirely. Slowly he turns, exposing his round face, sunken eyes and bearded chin.

He looks down on us, raises an eyebrow suspiciously, smirks slightly then spins back around and steps aside for us to pass. That's when it hits me - The REAL McKEY! This hallway, that burly man, Tracy - it's the place that started it all. Still there is something out of sorts. Tracy looks at me; his light eyes squint questioningly. I return his gaze and shrug my shoulders.

Together we step out of the hallway into the establishment, which is packed to the gills with masses upon masses of what I assume to be citizens from Realm who have jumped the border illegally. What's missing is the usual banter, loud music and clanking of goblets and beer bottles you normally hear in a bar.

Instead all the occupants are sitting or standing, silently watching a clip on the dusty old television set mounted in the back corner of the room. There are images of a volcano erupting, emitting a steady stream of black smoke into a darkened sky. The scenes flash across the screen then switch to a blonde newscaster sitting comfortably behind a news desk.

"What?...." Tracy begins as the reporter starts to speak. Everyone is silent, including the television set which is extremely frustrating. Why do all these people care about this volcano and why don't they actually want to hear what's going on? Along the bottom ticker I can just make out the words "Katla eruption - Iceland" before some commercial clicks on.

"I don't believe it!"

"Believe what?" I whine.

"Holy hell the volcano erupted!"

"So?"

"After all these years? I was beginning to think it would never happen – COULD never happen!"

"I still don't...."

"Lily, the volcano erupted! Do you know what this means?" Tracy's expression is a combination of surprise and relief. I, on the other hand, am feeling annoyed.

"Obviously not!"

"Oh my god, I still don't believe it!"

"For crying out loud Tracy! - What does it mean?"

"It means..."

"Yeah?"

"The King..."

"What about him?"

"He's dead!"

Find out what happens next in Book 3,
Realm: Battle For The Throne

Printed in Great Britain
by Amazon